Thank goodness he'd never given into any errant urges to have sex with her, because he was certain that would have ruined the best relationship he'd ever had with a woman.

If Sophie weren't his assistant, she might have been the perfect woman for him. Low-maintenance, undemanding, not at all clingy. Max, however, had Sophie's number. Underneath that practical veneer, she was a romantic at heart. With his past disastrous relationships with women, he'd learned to steer clear of ones who wanted romance and home and hearth. Even though she'd followed him around the world, Max had an itchy, uncomfortable feeling that Sophie wanted a husband and a baby—to go along with that dog she was always talking about getting.

And the romantic in Sophie was now pushing him to go to the land of his newly revealed royal relatives.

"You're never going to stop with this until I visit Chantaine," he said. "Are you?"

She looked at him with unapologetic determination. "Never. Ever."

"Okay, I'll go," he said, trying to avoid her slight smile.

Because she looked as if she knew something he didn't. That wasn't a good thing.

Dear Reader,

Welcome to Chantaine, a lovely Mediterranean island where the royal Devereaux rule and fall in love. When Max Carter learns his biological father was Prince Edward Devereaux, he's not impressed. Adopted as a baby, Max has been raised to make his own way. These days, he's known for the impressive bridges and roads he constructs all over the world, and he couldn't care less about any biological ties he may have to a bunch of royals.

When his longtime assistant, Sophie Taylor, guilts him into meeting his new half siblings, he learns how much the Devereaux care for their country and their people. He finds himself drawn into using his expertise to help improve Chantaine.

More important, Max learns he may need to rethink his attitude about keeping his distance from people, especially when his assistant, Sophie, gains the attention of a palace advisor. Sophie was the best assistant Max had ever employed and he'd always been careful to keep their relationship friendly, but not romantic.

On the other hand, Sophie has hidden her mile-wide crush from Max from the first day she fell for him. As she's grown to know him more throughout the past few years, she despairs that he'll never return her feelings.

Feelings can change in lots of ways when Sophie and Max give in to their passion and Sophie gets pregnant. Max may be ready to make a commitment, but Sophie wants more than papers. She wants love!

I would love to hear from you if you get a chance to read *How to Catch a Prince.* You can email me at leannebbb@aol.com.

Happy reading,

Leanne

HOW TO CATCH A PRINCE

LEANNE BANKS

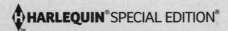
HARLEQUIN® SPECIAL EDITION®

Recycling programs
for this product may
not exist in your area.

ISBN-13: 978-0-373-65729-2

HOW TO CATCH A PRINCE

Printed in U.S.A.

Books by Leanne Banks

LEANNE BANKS

is a *New York Times* and *USA TODAY* bestselling author who is surprised every time she realizes how many books she has written. Leanne loves chocolate, the beach and new adventures. To name a few, Leanne has ridden on an elephant, stood on an ostrich egg (no, it didn't break), and gone parasailing and indoor skydiving. Leanne loves writing romance because she believes in the power and magic of love. She lives in Virginia with her family and a four-and-a-half-pound Pomeranian named Bijou. Visit her website, www.leannebanks.com.

This book is dedicated to my husband, Tony Banks, for his unswerving belief in me and for all the take-out food he has brought me during deadlines.

Chapter One

"**Y**ou have to go," Sophie Taylor insisted for the tenth time.

Glancing out the window of his temporary office trailer, Max Carter felt a sense of satisfaction at the sight of the finished bridge project. The new construction gleamed in the Australian sun as if it were shouting *success*.

"I've got too much to do," he said, turning to face his assistant of four years. "Paperwork, then it's on to the next project."

Sophie scowled at him. "You could take a short break. It's near the holidays. It wouldn't kill you. I can't believe you're dismissing this without giving it a second thought. They're your family."

Max rolled his eyes. There were few people he'd allow

to argue with him this much, but Sophie had proven her value to him time and time again. He couldn't think of another woman he respected more. Even now as she frowned at him with softly accusing chocolate-brown eyes from behind her smudged glasses, he felt compelled to listen to her. He knew that beneath that curly mass of hair, she had a quick and fair mind.

"Why do you care so much about this? It's not *your* family," he said.

"I don't want you to have any regrets."

He sighed, remembering the day the two representatives of the Royal House of Devereaux had hunted him down on the job site. The words they'd said to him had been stuck in his brain like the annoying refrain of a song he couldn't make go away.

Your biological father was Prince Edward of Chantaine.

"They're not my family, Sophie. I can't believe these royals are thrilled with the news that their father hatched a couple of extra children with a B-movie actress in America." Although Max had always known he was adopted, he never would have dreamed his biological parents were a prince and actress!

"What about Coco Jordan?" Sophie asked, referring to the other child the prince and actress had produced. "She's your sister. Don't you at least want to meet her? And, who knows, maybe she wants to meet you. You might try thinking about the feelings of someone other than yourself. Didn't you say both of your parents had passed away? She has no one now. No one except you."

"She doesn't have me," he retorted, but he felt an itchy sensation of obligation. "I wouldn't be able to pick her out of a crowd of two."

Her frown deepened. "Maybe you should just give her a chance."

Max sighed and glanced around the trailer that had become his temporary office and home. The LEGO rendering of the bridge sat next to his desk. A small Christmas tree blinked in the corner. Two stuffed puppies sat next to Sophie's desk. Sophie had complained many times over that she wanted a dog, but there was no way she could drag a pet to all the places Max had taken her for projects, many of which were international. From the first time she'd assisted him on a job, he'd learned she was the best assistant he could possibly have despite her complaints. He grumbled and she helped fix things. She anticipated his needs. Thank goodness he'd never given into any errant urges to have sex with her because he was certain that would have ruined the best relationship he'd ever had with a woman.

If she weren't his assistant, she might have been the perfect woman for him. Low-maintenance, undemanding and she wasn't at all clingy. Max, however, had Sophie's number. Underneath that practical veneer, Sophie was a romantic at heart. Even though she'd followed him around the world, he had an itchy, uncomfortable feeling that Sophie wanted a husband and baby to go along with that dog she so desired.

And with his past disastrous relationships with women, he'd learned to steer clear of women who wanted romance and home and hearth. "You're never gonna stop with this until I visit Chantaine," he said. "Are you?"

She looked at him from behind her glasses with unapologetic determination. "Never. Ever."

"Okay. I'll go," he said. "For one day. Just one day and then you don't get to look at me with that guilty face."

Sophie gave a slight smile. "One day will be enough."

Max felt a sinking feeling at her expression. She looked like she knew something he didn't. That wasn't a good thing.

Max left the following day for the island country of Chantaine to meet his new relatives while Sophie wrapped up the loose ends of the contract. Terri Caldwell, one of the other assistants on the project, walked into the trailer.

"How's it going?"

"I'm halfway through a million pages of paperwork," Sophie said without looking up from her laptop.

"That's what you get for being so efficient and devoted," Terri teased. "And head over heels for Max Carter."

Sophie grimaced. Nearly a decade older than herself, Terri was a good woman from Arkansas, honest to a fault. Her husband was a truck driver back in the States, but they visited every chance they got. Terri had started taking the long-distance work to pay for her twin boys' college tuition. She had become a good friend to Sophie especially during the last couple of months. Terri was intuitive enough to spot Sophie's unrequited feelings for Max, and Sophie had grown to trust the woman's discretion. It had been a relief to have the older woman's sympathy. "Don't rub it in. I'll get over him someday. Maybe someday soon. I really want a King Charles spaniel and there's no way I can do that if I allow him to keep dragging me all over the world."

"What amazes me is that he doesn't seem to notice your feelings for him when everyone else can see it as plain as day," Terri said, leaning against Sophie's desk.

Sophie felt a jagged twist inside her. "He doesn't see me as a woman. He sees me as the ultimate assistant."

"Well, you are the ultimate assistant," Terri agreed with a nod. "But you're also a woman. Ever thought about giving him a clue about that?"

Sophie stopped keying in the final construction details and glanced up at Terri. "I'm not exactly sure how. I'm not the type to wear low-cut shirts or short skirts. Or lots of makeup. But I'm still feminine."

"Of course you are. I wonder if Max might belly up to the bar if he had a little competition."

Sophie shook her head. "That's not my way."

"Sometimes men need a little push. You may have to think outside the box. Unless you're okay with having unrequited love for the rest of your life."

Sophie sighed, remembering the first time she'd met Max. She'd been bowled over. He was the Indiana Jones of road construction. She'd quickly learned how to anticipate his professional needs. He'd learned, not quite as quickly, how valuable she could be to him. Though her feelings for him had deepened over the years, only his professional respect had grown for her, and nothing more.

Sophie had hoped and wished, but nothing romantic had developed between them. She'd watched Max engage in several quickie affairs that had brought her enormous pain. Somehow, his relationship with her had turned out to be his most long-lasting one with a woman. Except, he didn't really view her as a *woman*.

"Maybe with the holiday break, I can go back home and get my King Charles spaniel. Maybe then I'll get over him," Sophie said. "Not being around him could help me get over him."

"It would help if he weren't so good-looking," Terri said.

"I can get over the good-looking part, but he can be charming," Sophie said. "When he wants to be, he can be so damn charming."

"He can also be a toad. He's fine about making us all work long hours" Terri said.

"True, but he works longer than anyone else. And everyone is well-compensated. The real trouble for me is that he is charitable. He puts on this front about only caring about himself, but everywhere we go, he gets the crew involved in some kind of charity project." She pointed at the pile of wrapped gifts next to the Christmas tree. "For children stuck in the hospital over the holidays. If only he were as selfish and uncaring as he says he is."

"Have you gone out with another man since you've met Max?" Terri asked.

Self-consciousness burned through her. "Yes, I have," she said. "Four times. All during my vacations."

"Woo-hoo. Four times in four years." Terri shook her head. "I dare you to meet six new men over your holiday."

"How am I supposed to do that?"

"Online. You can arrange meet-ups in no time."

"I think I'd rather poke out my eye with a pencil," Sophie said under her breath.

"You gotta do something," Terri said. "You either need to pull that pony in or let him ride."

Max couldn't see much of the island country of Chantaine while soaring in the sky since he was arriving after dark. He'd run a computer search and caught a few images. Beautiful country that seemed to combine Greece's Mediterranean views, France's sophistication and Italy's charm. While he'd run the search, he'd also looked into his new so-called siblings. The eldest, Crown Prince Stefan, came across as a hard worker, more serious-minded than their biological father, Prince Edward. It appeared that their father had enjoyed yachting and living like a playboy, much more than ruling.

Max figured that his adopted parents' failed marriage was one more reason for him to never get married. They had fought more than they hadn't when his father had been around. When things got tough, which was quite frequent, his adoptive father would leave the house and desert Max's adoptive mother. He'd always been grateful for the home and opportunities his parents had provided for him, but their discord had bothered him the first time he'd heard them screaming at each other and doors slamming at night.

Now, Max not only had been given a bad example of marriage, he had the genetic material of a philanderer from Prince Edward.

He'd briefly checked out the rest of the Devereaux clan. The eldest sister, Valentina, lived in Texas with her rancher husband and their daughter. The second sister, Fredericka, lived in France with her movie producer husband. Princess Bridget was married to a doctor from the States and Princess Pippa had just married an international businessman. The youngest brother, Jacques, attended Oxford and played soccer.

Once he'd told the palace he would be coming, Prince Stefan's wife, Eve, had sent him a message asking him to keep his visit secret because she wanted his presence to be a surprise for Coco Jordan's wedding. The idea that he would be a surprise for anyone's wedding, let alone his full-blooded sister, made him squeamish, but he agreed to the plan.

The plane landed with a jolt, reminding him he was about to put himself in an insane situation. He thought of how Sophie had hounded him. After this brief visit, she wouldn't be able to look at him with her guilt gaze. Lord knew, he hated that guilt gaze.

A man approached him at the luggage carousel. "Mr. Carter? Mr. Maxwell Carter?"

Max nodded slowly. "Yes, and you?"

"I'm Mr. Bernard, an assistant to His Highness,

Prince Stefan. We're happy that you're visiting Chantaine. Welcome to our country. If it pleases you, I have a driver ready to take you to a villa just outside the palace grounds. We would normally invite you to stay on the palace grounds itself, but with Miss Jordan's wedding taking place in a few days, Princesses Eve and Bridget have requested to keep your presence secret until the nuptials."

"Fine with me," he said reluctantly, and realized his one-day stay had just been extended.

Three days later, after several tours of the island, Max was escorted to the office of Crown Prince Stefan Devereaux. Now, pacing the office as he waited for his half brother, Prince Stefan, he felt the hard gaze of the palace security tracking every move he made. If the Devereauxes were so insistent that he join them, then why did they look at him as if he were a potential assassin?

One moment later, a man stepped inside the room. "His Royal Highness, Prince Stefan," the man announced.

A dark-haired man wearing a black suit strode toward him and nodded. "Maxwell Carter?"

Max nodded. "Yes. Max. And what shall I call you? Your highness or Prince Stefan?"

Prince Stefan lifted his left eyebrow. "Stefan will do."

Max nodded again. "Stefan it is."

Stefan waved his hand to a chair facing the desk and then sank into the large chair behind the desk. "I appreciate that you have made an effort to come to Coco

Jordan's wedding. Coco has made a huge effort to meet us...and now to meet you."

Max shrugged, uncomfortable with Stefan's gratitude. He'd expected the man to be more cold and pompous. "I haven't met any members of the family before now."

"You will before and after the ceremony," Stefan promised, glancing at his watch. "In fact, the girls should be stopping by any minute. My sisters have been fussing over Coco for the last few days. I'm sure you're curious to meet her."

"I suppose," Max said. "I have no idea what kind of person she is even though we share the same blood."

"Well, she's delightful," Stefan said. "Kind and compassionate. The kind of woman you would want as a sister."

"I'm impressed that you can say that after you have four sisters."

Stefan laughed. "Good point. My sisters do their best to keep me in line."

"And you?" Max asked.

"I do my best to keep them out of the equation," Stefan said. "I'm told you've had a chance to tour the island?"

Max nodded. "I have," he said. "It's a beautiful place, and because of my profession I notice the infrastructure. Most of the roads and bridges are in good condition except the north end of the island."

"I was going to ask you about that," Stefan said. "One of my brothers-in-law has expressed an interest in building a green retreat with an emphasis on the nature areas on that part of the island, but he and I agree that the roads currently can't sustain the possibility. We'd like to improve the roads, but keep the costs down."

"Isn't this something your government would pursue? I wouldn't have expected a royal to have interest in roads."

Stefan gave a shark-like smile. "Then you wouldn't be familiar with the current generation of Devereauxes. All of us are interested about improving our country and the life of our citizens."

"Unlike previous generations?" he asked, thinking of his biological father, who, from everything he'd read, was a shameless playboy.

Stefan's facial expression closed. "Every generation has their emphasis. We can either be inspired by what they did or didn't do or spend our lives complaining about it. I sense that you're a man of action rather than the kind to sit around grumbling. Perhaps we have that in common."

A knock sounded on the door and Stefan's assistant opened it. Three women stepped inside the room. Two of them were very pregnant. The one who was not pregnant stepped toward him. "Oh, you must be Maxwell Carter. We're so thrilled you could make it for Coco's wedding. She'll be so excited."

"This is my sister Bridget," Stefan said. "She loves to create surprises for family members."

One of the pregnant women with wild hair laughed lightly and extended her hand. "Very true. I'm Phillipa and very pleased to meet you. Thank you for coming."

Stefan slid his arm around the back of the other very pregnant woman. "This is my wife. Princess Eve."

Not exactly sure how to address the roomful of royals, Max nodded. "Your highnesses," he said.

Eve extended her hand. "Titles are unnecessary," she said with a hint of a twang that made Max recall she was from the States. "As everyone has said, we're just very pleased that you were able to come."

He found it odd how protective the Devereauxes were of their father's illegitimate child, Coco. "If you don't mind my saying so, you haven't known Coco very long. It's surprising how attached you seem to be to her," he said.

Eve smiled gently. "Ah, well, you'll understand when you meet her. She is such a kind soul."

"Wouldn't take advantage of anyone," Bridget added.

"Very sweet and so alone in the world since her mother died," Phillipa said.

"Except now she has her husband and his daughter," Bridget pointed out.

"Family means so much to her, and she really had none," Eve said. "We couldn't resist her after we met her."

"We don't have much time," Bridget said. "Apologies, but we do have a plan for when we'd like to introduce you at the reception. We'll have you sit in the back of the chapel so you won't miss the wedding."

"Because every man loves a wedding," Stefan muttered dryly.

Both Bridget and Phillipa scowled at their brother,

and at that moment, Max felt a strange kinship with Stefan.

Stefan shrugged. "What? It's not as if a wedding is like a soccer match."

An hour later, Max sat in the back of the chapel feeling incredibly uncomfortable. He watched as his full-blooded sister met her groom and both of them pronounced their vows. The Devereaux sisters crowded around the couple, and Max felt a strange twist in his chest. His sister's voice touched something deep inside him. The Devereauxes were kinder than he'd expected. Why had the royals decided Coco belonged to him? Why had Coco pursued both the Devereauxes and him?

Max watched as the groom kissed his so-called sister and felt another bizarre clench in his gut. Why did this sight affect him? Why did he care?

After the couple kissed, Max was led to a reception in the ballroom. Then Bridget offered him a drink. "I hope whiskey is okay," she said. "I never know what you Yanks want."

Max downed the drink. "Whiskey's fine. What's the plan?"

"Just tell Coco how glad you are to meet her and how special she is. If you knew her, it wouldn't be difficult," she said.

"As you wish, your highness," he said and put his empty glass on a tray.

"You're missing out," Bridget said. "But you'll have to learn that on your own. Come along."

She led him to the bride and groom. He stared into his sister's face. He kept trying to tell himself that Coco wasn't his real sister, but he felt a sense of connection with her.

She stared at him. "You're my brother, aren't you?"

"Yes, and you're my sister. Maxwell Carter at your service, your highness," he said in a wry voice.

She laughed out loud. "Yes, just as you are a prince, your highness."

"Not me," he said, shaking his head, feeling regret steep through him. "I wish I'd known you before."

He saw the same wisp of loss he felt slide through her. "You know me now and I'll be your pain in the butt sister for the rest of your life."

"Why do I feel like I won the genetic lottery?" Max asked.

Her groom, Benjamin, stepped forward. "Because you did, in every way." And then he took Coco's mouth in a kiss.

Arriving back for a holiday visit in Northern Virginia, at her mother's home, Sophie braced herself for her mother's usual inquisition. This time, however, her mother seemed to have given up on nagging Sophie to get married. Her mother was far more relaxed than Sophie could remember. As a single parent, Katherine Taylor had spent most of Sophie's growing-up years in fear of losing her job and subsequently being unable to care for Sophie. It had taken years for Katherine to trust Sophie to be able to take care of herself, but now it appeared her mother believed.

Sophie did her best to push Max and his situation from her mind. She needed some downtime. Even with the rush of decorating and baking, she found herself easing into a routine and taunting herself with advertisements for dogs.

After roaming the globe with Max for years, she wondered if she was ready for a different job. Although being away from Max was less exciting, she found herself much more calm and at peace. Maybe it was time to find a place of her own where she could stay for more than a few weeks at a time. The possibility was seductive, but something kept her from calling the engineering firm that employed her.

On New Year's Day, she began composing a list of resolutions. The first was that she was going to start having a life, wherever she lived. As she recalled her list, her cell phone rang and she saw the caller ID. Max. Her stomach danced with stupid anticipation. She pressed the answer button. "Yes, Sophie."

"Okay, I met my sister. She was nice. You were right. But I ended up staying a lot longer than one day. This Prince Stefan guy is a shark. That said, he needs a road fixed. Our company loves the idea of fixing the roads of an exotic island country, so we have our new assignment. I want you to come to Chantaine."

"What? I thought I was going to get some vacation time," she said.

"I'll give you some time off when you're here in Chantaine. You'll like it here," he said.

Sophie sighed, wondering if this was when she should finally say no to Max. It had been a fun ride traveling to exotic places to work with him, but she was longing for a home of her own. She was tired of feeling unsettled. "When would you need me?" she asked.

"Yesterday. Sophie, come on. You know what a great team we are. We always get the job done ahead of time and under budget when we're working together. There's no one I can count on the same way I can count on you."

Sophie took a deep breath and said what she always said to Max. "Okay." But this was going to be the last time. Really.

Two days later, Sophie gaped out the window of the jet as it neared the island. She couldn't believe how beautiful the island of Chantaine was. White sandy beach on one side, rocky mountains on the other with azure ocean surrounding it all. Australia had been amazing. She'd been lucky enough to steal a long weekend over to New Zealand and absorb the lush gorgeousness of that island. But this, she thought, this was incredible. Paradise. She couldn't wait to see it on the ground. Within moments, the plane landed. She grabbed her carry-on from the overhead compartment and waited her turn to exit the plane.

Her checked luggage arrived without a hitch. Nice change, given how many times the airlines had lost it in the past. She walked outside the terminal to what felt like a perfect combination of temperature and humidity and thought she would never want to leave this place.

A Mercedes slid in front of her. The driver and Max exited at the same time. "Miss," the driver said.

"Sophie," Max said. "We've got work to do."

"I expected that. But you mentioned vacation days."

"You'll get a break. Just not right away."

"Great," she muttered under her breath. After the long flight, she didn't have the energy to put up a fight.

The driver relieved her of her luggage and opened the car door for her. Sophie was grateful for the consideration. "Thank you," she said, climbing into the car.

"The island is so beautiful," she said to Max as he followed her.

"Yes, but the north side is a mess. That's where we'll be working. Unstable roads. Rock slides. Not acceptable. Far too dangerous. Stefan thinks one of his brother-in-laws will want to build a resort there, but the roads will have to be improved."

"Will they need a bridge?" she asked.

"I think we can just build up the road. It's tricky because it's hard to get materials the second you want them."

"Which will drive you crazy," she said. "Since you consider patience a vice."

Max shrugged. "You know me," he said while lowering his window so that the breeze flowed through the backseat. "My impatience is my strength and weakness. I try to direct it toward my strength as much as possible."

Sophie nodded. "What do you think of your new relatives?"

He moved his head from side to side. "An interesting crew."

"I'm surprised you agreed to direct this road construction for them," she said.

"Why not? Plus, if I do this, I won't feel obligated to do anything else."

Surprised, she threw a questioning glance at him. "Obligated?" she echoed.

"It's a weird situation," he said. "I'm related to them, but I don't feel like I am. I wouldn't feel right just doing nothing."

"Hmm," she said. "So this is a guilt job?"

He shrugged. "An obligatory job," he said. "And the good thing is that the company will pay for it."

Sophie took a deep breath. "You mentioned that Prince Stefan is a shark. You sure sound like one at the moment."

"I haven't figured them out. Stefan has royal manners, but underneath, he can be a hard case. He married an American and she's about to give birth. Come to think of it, she's Texan and so are two of the sisters' husbands. He seems to truly love his wife. The same for the other couples I met."

"You sound astonished," she said.

"I'm not used to it. My parents spent most of their time fighting when my dad was home. He spent most of the time on the road."

Sophie studied him for a long moment. Although Max

had alluded to the fact that his parents hadn't shared a great relationship, he'd never come right out and said it until now. It was eye-opening.

"You know, some people actually do fall in love, get married and stay in love," she said.

"Sounds like a fairy tale to me," he said, staring out the window as the car rode past one of the most spectacular beaches Sophie had ever seen.

"I knew you were cynical about romance, but—"

"It's not cynical," he said. "It's realistic. The reason men and women marry is for sex. Then children. Men want children for progeny's sake. Ego. The focus temporarily turns to children. Then men need to feel young again and sex is key. Even with the help from the blue pill."

She slid him a sideways glance. "Blue pill. What do you know about that?"

He chuckled. "I don't need it yet."

"You and I have never really discussed your attitude toward marriage. You've given little clues, but I've never heard your complete scientific view."

"Scientific?" he echoed.

"You're an engineer. It's coming through in your opinion."

"It's not just an opinion," he said. "It's based on observation and scientific research," he said.

"Uh-huh, then how do you explain the way Prince Stefan acts toward his wife?"

"It won't last. They're in the progeny stage."

Sophie's heart sank. After all these years, she was beginning to believe that there was no hope for Max. He truly didn't believe in love.

Chapter Two

One jam-packed week later, Sophie felt a terrible dip in her stomach as she lifted her gaze to look at Max. "What do you mean? The Devereaux women want to meet me? Why?"

"The Devereaux women got curious when I told them about you. The only way to satisfy their interest is for you to meet them," Max told her almost apologetically as he looked around the working trailer.

Sophie narrowed her eyes. "What did you tell them about me?"

He shrugged and shoved his hands into his pockets. "Just that you're the best assistant ever. And brilliant."

She rolled her eyes. "Nothing you would ever say to my face, of course."

"That's not true. I told you that you were my best assistant ever."

"Hmm," she said. "When is this meeting supposed to take place?"

"Tomorrow," he said.

Sophie thought about her hair and her wardrobe. She scowled. "How am I supposed to get ready for a meeting with royals in twenty-four hours?"

"It's not a big deal. Just tea," he said.

"Tea?" she repeatd. "Do you know what that involves?"

He shrugged. "It can't be that much of a big deal," he said.

"Did you promise that I would attend?"

Max almost squirmed. And he never squirmed. "Sure," he said. "They were pressing and I thought you would like the break."

"Break?" she said. "Do you really think meeting royalty for tea would be a *break?*"

"Well, it's not like keeping the workers in line—"

Sophie lifted her hand to cut him off and shook her head. "Forget it," she said. "I'm leaving for the day."

"Now?" he asked, clearly surprised.

"Yes, now," she said. "I'm meeting royalty tomorrow and I have nothing to wear."

"But I wanted you to recheck the stats on—"

She shook her head. "Not happening today," she said as she shut down her laptop. "See you the day after tomorrow."

Sophie knew she wasn't just frustrated about meeting the Deveraux family at short notice. She was also crazy out of her head that Max still didn't see her as a woman, even in such a beautiful and romantic setting. During the last month, she had worked her butt off over twelve hours a day, side by side with Max, but he still hadn't seemed to notice her.

"Whoa," Max said.

"Exactly," she retorted as she headed for the door. "Whoa."

Sophie slammed the door behind her and headed for her teeny, tiny car. She started the car, put it in gear and took the winding road down the mountain. Despite her impatience with Max, she appreciated the challenge of their project. Once they fixed these roads, everyone in Chantaine could enjoy the north end of the island where the vegetation and birds flourished.

This area almost resembled the jungle while most of the rest of the island featured rocky beaches and green parks. Every day during the last thirty-one days, Sophie had wondered if she should have refused Max's invitation to join him in Chantaine. She had wanted one last chance with Max, but now she was feeling regrets. Every day of being with him was driving her crazy.

Sophie sucked in a deep breath of the clean island air and sped down the winding road toward town. The drive took nearly an hour, but she was glad to be in the center of Chantaine with its variety of restaurants, entertainment and shopping, even though she rarely took part in what it had to offer.

In contrast, shopping was definitely in her future

today. She could not think of one thing in her wardrobe appropriate for a tea. She grabbed a bite to eat then focused on finding a new dress and planned to charge Max for the purchase. He should have given her more notice, the jerk.

After zipping through several stores, she found a blue dress that fit and flattered. The price tag made her wince, but was soon forgotten as she headed to a hair salon. It had been over a month since her curly hair had been shaped.

After her hair appointment, Sophie was exhausted and dragged herself back to her apartment. Washing her face and brushing her teeth, she pulled on a nightgown, cursing Max until she fell asleep.

Sophie slept in the next morning, but when she awakened, she immediately felt panicky. She showered and fussed with her hair and makeup. Too soon, however, her cell rang with the news that a driver would pick her up to bring her to the palace.

Sophie's stomach dipped again. She tried to recall everything Max had said about his half sisters, the princesses, but it all jumbled with her facts and figures about the road project. She leaned her head against the seat back and tried to relax as the driver took her inside the palace gates.

Seconds later, however, the driver let her out at the palace entrance. A man met her and guided her inside. "Miss Taylor?"

"Yes, thank you," she said. "It's beautiful."

"Thank you," he said. "We think so, too. I'll take you

to the room where you will share tea with the princesses of Devereaux."

"Thank you," she said, but wasn't so sure about all this. "So, how do you like living in Chantaine?" she asked nervously.

The man glanced at her. "I like it very much," he said.

Of course, she thought. What else was he going to say? It sucks dirtwater? She nodded, trying to calm her nerves.

He led her into a beautifully decorated parlor with a table readied for formal tea.

"Ma'am, are you all right?" a man asked from behind her.

Sophie whipped around to face the man at the door. "Yes, of course," she said. "I'm Sophie. And you are?"

"Walter Deneuve," the man said. "You looked a bit pale."

Sophie bit her lip. "I'm a little nervous. I've never had tea with a bunch of royals."

Walter smiled. "The Devereauxes are quite welcoming. I think you'll enjoy them."

"Thank you," she said, but still wasn't sure. "The pastries look delicious," she said and wandered around the table.

A half moment later Walter stood at attention, the door opened, and three women entered the room, two of which were waddling in late pregnancy.

"Her Highness, Princess Eve, wife of Crown Prince Stefan," Walter announced.

Sophie dipped her head.

"Her Highnesses Bridget and Phillipa," he continued.

"Yes, yes, enough of that," Eve said in a Texas drawl as she extended her hand. "I'm Eve and at least thirteen months pregnant. Very pleased to meet you. I'm sorry Maxwell didn't bring you around sooner."

Sophie smiled and shook Eve's hand. "Thank you. And I hope your delivery is quick and smooth."

"Me, too," Eve said in a grumbly voice.

"I'm Bridget and I'm not pregnant," the dark-haired woman wearing high heels said cheerfully. "But I've also adopted twin toddler boys."

"You're brave," Sophie couldn't help saying.

Bridget laughed. "I like you already. This is Phillipa, but we call her Pippa. Her delivery date is right behind Eve's."

Sophie met the kind gaze of the youngest princess. "It's nice to meet you. I hope you, too, have a quick and smooth delivery."

Pippa beamed. "Thank you. I'm hoping for the same."

"Shall we sit?" Eve asked. "These days, I'm always happy to sit."

"Of course," Bridget said and led the way to the table.

Eve glanced at Sophie. "I don't really like hot tea. Would you like iced tea?"

Sophie felt an easing inside her. "I would love some iced tea."

Soon enough, sandwiches and pastries were served.

"What is it like working with Maxwell? He seems very intense," Bridget said, taking a bite of a pastry.

He's a pain in the butt, Sophie thought, but bit her tongue. "You're right. He's very intense. Type A."

"Yes, he's mentioned you several times, and it occurred to me that you might enjoy some female companionship. I hear there aren't many women on the construction site," Eve said, then smiled. "Then again, maybe you enjoy being surrounded by all those men."

Sophie laughed at the thought. "Perhaps I would in a different situation, but there's no flirting. It's all about getting the job done."

"Well, that's a shame," Bridget said, pursing her lips. "Perhaps we can help find someone to amuse Sophie during her off-hours."

Pippa groaned. "Oh, no. You're not going to start matchmaking again."

"I'm determined to succeed one of these days," Bridget said.

The resolve in Bridget's voice made Sophie a little uneasy. "Not necessary. I can amuse myself. Besides, it's not as if I'll have that much free time."

"Well, everyone needs a break now and then. So I've been told repeatedly," Eve said with a sigh.

Bridget nodded. "Eve hasn't had the easiest pregnancy, so we've all had to help her accept that she can't keep going at breakneck speed. Coco was especially helpful getting through to Eve."

At the mention of Max's full-blood sister, Sophie felt a twist of curiosity. "Max hasn't discussed her much, but she sounds like a very sweet person."

"Oh, she is," Pippa said. "We would kidnap her and make her live in Chantaine if possible."

"I would have liked to have met her," Sophie said.

"Perhaps you will," Pippa said. "Once Eve and I have our babies, I know she'll be dying to see them."

"In the meantime, you'll have to come visit my ranch," Bridget said with a sly sense of pride.

"Ranch?" Sophie echoed.

"Yes, my husband is originally from Texas. He is the official medical director for Chantaine and I noticed that he was missing his home state, so we've built a ranch for him. We have chickens, horses and now we even have two cows. So you'll feel totally at home on our ranch."

Sophie swallowed a chuckle. She hadn't spent one day of her life on a ranch. "It sounds fabulous. How did you do it?"

"Trust me, it wasn't easy and it's taken months, but my husband seems happier, so that makes me happy. The only thing that would please him more is if Chantaine had a semi-professional baseball team. I don't think that's going to happen."

"Where are you from?" Eve asked, shifting her weight as if she were uncomfortable. Sophie felt sorry for the woman. She was probably always uncomfortable at this stage of her pregnancy.

"The Washington, D.C., area," she said.

Eve blinked then snickered. "Sophie is from the city, Bridget. Not everyone from America is from Texas."

Bridget frowned for a moment then her face brightened. "No problem. Perhaps Sophie and I could take a quick trip to Paris and we could visit Fredericka, one of our sisters."

Both Pippa and Eve gave loud sounds of disapproval. "Not before we deliver," Eve said. "If we're trapped here on the island, then you have to stay, too."

"Trapped in paradise?" Bridget echoed with a cheeky smile. "Who would possibly call it trapped?"

"You're the one taking off for Italy and France every chance you get. You just wait until you get pregnant and your husband gets all protective of you," Eve said. "You'll be singing a different song."

"With twin toddlers, I won't be getting pregnant any-time soon," Bridget promised.

Pippa glanced at Sophie. "We must stop with all this baby talk. We're probably boring our guest to death."

"Oh, no," Sophie said. "It's a nice change from discussions about rocks and engineering."

"From what Max has said, it sounds as if he does a lot of traveling," Eve said. "Do you enjoy it?"

"For the most part, I do," Sophie said. "It's fascinating to see places that were just spots on a map to me. But all this travel prevents me from getting a dog."

Bridget nodded. "My husband feels the same way. A dog is next on our list as soon as the boys are toilet trained."

More courses of fruits and sweets were served. After a while of chatting and giggling, the man who'd been standing by the door the entire time walked toward Eve and spoke to her in a low voice. Eve nodded. "Thank you. I asked Walter to remind me when Stephenia is supposed to wake up from her nap. I promised her a trip to the playground. She's missing the boys since you moved out."

"I'll bring them soon," Bridget said. "I've just wanted them to get adjusted to *the ranch*."

Bridget said it with such irony that Sophie couldn't conceal a chuckle.

Eve rose. "We must do this again."

Bridget nodded. "Or better yet, let's do lunch and shop."

"I'll agree to lunch, but no shopping for me," Eve said.

"Same here," Pippa said as the rest of them rose to their feet.

"Thank you so much for inviting me. I didn't know what to expect, but I have to say this is the most fun I've had in a long time," Sophie said, surprising herself a little with the realization.

The chauffeur met her at the palace door and drove her back to her apartment. It occurred to Sophie as the car wove through the picturesque streets that she'd been spending a lot of time working and hardly any time enjoying herself. For what reason? So she could be close to Max. Because she was still hoping he would notice her and fall madly in love with her.

Sophie caught a glimpse of the ocean and realized that she hadn't gone to the beach once since she'd arrived in Chantaine. Irritation niggled through her. Why was she staying with Max until the wee hours of the night if he wasn't going to notice her? It wasn't as if they accomplished much after dinnertime anyway.

She'd recently been reading a self-help book a co-worker from Australia had given her for Christmas. The book had supplied a quote that was sticking, annoyingly, in her head. *If you always do what you've always done, you'll always get what you've always gotten.*

Sophie frowned. What she'd *gotten* the last few years had been an adventurous job with great pay and an unrequited crush on Max. And no dog.

Sophie brooded over that for several moments.

The chauffeur surprised her, opening the door. "Miss?"

She hadn't even noticed the car had stopped. "Yes. Thank you for the ride."

"My pleasure," he said and helped her out of the car. That was nice, she thought. Someone treating her like a woman.

Sophie cringed. *Someone paid to treat her like a woman.*

Okay, that was it. She needed to think about doing something different. Sophie took a deep breath. Sophie looked at her apartment then turned away. She needed a night out.

She meandered in a few shops until they closed then walked to a café, got a sandwich and did some people-watching. All the while, she found herself second-guessing her decision to come to Chantaine. Maybe she should have refused Max. What would have happened if she had? What would she be doing now?

Sighing, Sophie wandered out of the shop and stopped at the crosswalk to walk the few blocks to her apartment.

She waited until the light signaled that she could cross and stepped off of the curb.

Out of the corner of her eye, she glimpsed a cute bright yellow scooter whizzing around the corner just before it sent her flying through the air.

Later, hours, was it days? Sophie awakened to a blurry sight in front of her.

"Sophie," Max said. "Sophie, it's me, Max. How are you?"

She opened her mouth, but her throat felt so dry. She made a croaking sound.

"Thank God," he muttered. She felt his hand on hers.

"Max," she whispered, but her head throbbed. "What happened?"

"A scooter ran into you," he said.

She took a deep breath and tried to concentrate. A vague visual of a scooter rounding a corner crossed her mind. "Oh, yeah."

"You remember?"

She nodded. "I was walking the crosswalk and the scooter came out of nowhere. Am I okay?"

He squeezed her hand. "Yeah, you're fine. Just rest."

Sophie awakened later. She wasn't sure when, but the nurse met her gaze. "How are you, sweetie?" she said. "You've had a rough go of it."

"Are you from Australia?" Sophie asked, taking in the accent of the nurse.

The woman nodded and smiled. "No. New Zealand. Both would be extremely offended."

Sophie smiled, but her body felt as if it ached all over. "Is anything broken?"

The nurse shook her head. "Your body is fine. We're still checking your brain."

"Oh, no," Sophia said. "Am I brain-damaged?"

The nurse shook her head. "A little confused," she said and tucked a blanket around Sophie. "Time will tell how confused."

Sophie frowned, feeling frightened. What did that mean? What if she couldn't perform her job? Worrying over the terrible possibilities, she felt a spurt of relief as Max walked into her room.

"Hi," she said. "So, am I brain-damaged?"

"No more than usual," he said then slid his hand over her forehead. "According to all the tests, you should be okay."

"How's the scooter driver?" she asked.

He smiled. "Unfortunately, better than you are."

Sophie scowled at him. "That sucks."

"Can't disagree, but he is too sorry for words. Been standing in the waiting room since you first arrived."

"Hmm," she said.

"I'm just glad you're awake and intelligible," he said, leaning toward her.

"Have I been unintelligible?" she asked, far more concerned about that than being awake.

She watched Max take a deep swallow. He shook his head. "Never."

Sophie sank back on her pillow. "You lie like a dog."

* * *

Moments after Sophie fell asleep again, Max stepped outside her room and headed for the nurses' station. His stomach hadn't stopped knotting since he'd received the call about Sophie from the emergency room. "Are you sure Miss Taylor is okay? She keeps falling asleep."

The nurse pulled up Sophie's information on her computer screen. "All her tests are normal. Her vitals are excellent. It's a miracle she wasn't hurt worse. Her body is demanding more rest to recover from the trauma. She'll improve rapidly over the next few days. I wouldn't be surprised if the doctor allowed her to leave this afternoon."

"This afternoon?" he said, shocked. "But she only arrived night before last."

"There's no swelling in her brain. She'll just need someone to be with her for the first night."

"We can take care of that," a cultured feminine voice said from behind him.

Max glanced at the woman and immediately recognized her. Princess Bridget with a male assistant or bodyguard behind her.

"Your highness," the nurse said, giving a slight curtsey.

Bridget dipped her head. "Thank you, but not necessary. I would like a thorough update on Miss Sophie Taylor's condition. Good to see you, Maxwell, but I much prefer to visit in a different situation. Did I hear correctly that they're going to release her?"

"That's what the nurse said, but the doctor will make the final decision."

"You don't seem too keen about her going home," Bridget said.

"She's still sleeping a lot and I can't see her taking care of herself," he said.

"I have the perfect solution. We'll bring her to the palace. I would invite her to my ranch, but the boys are such hellions she'd never find any peace. Pippa's husband, Nic, is taking his last trip to the States. She had to force Nic to go. The only way he would agree was if she stayed at the palace. So, Pippa can provide company and there will be staff to wait on Sophie hand and foot."

Her generosity took him off guard. At the same time, he felt responsible for Sophie. He almost felt as if he should be the one take care of her since she really didn't know anyone else in Chantaine. "I don't know. I have to think about what would be best for Sophie."

She blinked at him. "She couldn't possibly get better care somewhere other than the palace." Bridget frowned. "Do you wish for your assistant to stay somewhere else?"

He paused a half beat, thinking he didn't want to get overly involved with the Devereauxes. He didn't want Sophie to get involved with them either. He'd thought all that would be necessary for Sophie would be to go to the tea and that would be the end of it. "I want her to be comfortable."

"We enjoyed your Sophie—"

Impatience shot through him. "She's not *my* Sophie. She's my assistant."

Bridget gave an equally impatient nod. "Very well. We enjoyed her very much during our tea and all of us would like to spend more time with her. And we insist she spend her recovery at the palace."

Max felt a bit more sympathy for Stefan. Bridget was pushy. He wondered if the rest of the Devereaux women were.

Chapter Three

"I'm fine," Sophie said as she stood beside her bed.

She could tell that Max was concerned that she would fall any minute. "Are you sure?" he asked.

She nodded as he extended his hand to steady her. For that crazy, tiny moment, she relished his touch. His hand was strong and assuring against hers. The doctor had released her with the condition that someone could check in on her throughout the first night.

"Yes, I'm okay," she said. "I'm sure I'd be fine staying by myself."

"That's not going to happen. If you don't want to go to the palace, we can make other arrangements," he said and she felt him studying her.

"I'm okay with it. Then I can say I've spent the night

at a royal palace," she said, smiling. "Besides, it will just be one night."

"Or two," he said.

She was surprised at his concern for her. "Is there something I haven't been told? Am I okay?" she asked. "Have I lost some of my mental capacity? What did the doctor say?"

"You're fine," he said and squeezed her shoulder. "The doctor said all your tests are normal."

"Then why are you being so weird?" she asked, searching his gaze.

He shook his head. "I was caught off guard. You're always so strong and to see you hurt, it—" He broke off. "It did something to me."

His concern rocked through her. "Thanks," she said. "But I think I'm going to be okay." She glanced at his face and corrected herself. "I know I'm going to be okay."

"You call me anytime you want to leave the palace," he said.

Again, she was surprised at his concern for her. "No problem. I don't think they'll throw me in the dungeon."

"Okay, I'm here if you need me. I'll ride with you to the palace," he said. "Bridget was very insistent that you should stay at the palace. She was…pushy."

Sophie couldn't help laughing. "You think?"

Max frowned.

"I'll be all better tomorrow, so it won't be an issue."

"Okay," he said and his gaze held hers.

With his outward expression of worry for her, she

could almost think she was emotionally important to him. Could that be possible?

Then he stepped away, and she immediately felt his absence.

The nurse entered the room. "All ready?" the woman asked.

Seconds later, a palace assistant appeared. "We're ready to escort Miss Taylor away."

"Here are the instructions," the nurse said, lifting them.

Max snatched the sheet of paper. "Can you make an extra copy?"

The nurse lifted her eyebrows. "Of course, sir."

Just a few moments later, Sophie was driven away from the hospital toward the palace with Max by her side. Sophie leaned her head back against the seat. "Those Devereauxes lead a different life."

She felt Max's gaze on her. "What?" she asked, not opening her eyes.

"Are you saying you would like to live like a royal?" he asked.

She opened her eyes and met his gaze. "I wouldn't mind living like a royal every once in a while," she said. "But not all the time. How's that royal thing working out for you?"

He frowned. "So far, no one is all that interested in me."

"That bothers you?" she asked.

"Hell, no," he said. "I think I understand my role with the Devereauxes. They're happy to use my resources to improve their island, and they're relieved I don't want anything from them."

"You may be partly right, but after meeting the Devereaux sisters, they seem like caring people. If you gave them half a chance, you might enjoy a nice relationship with them," she said.

"I'm giving them a good road. I'm sure they'll value that far more than being buddies with me."

"I wish you wouldn't be so stubborn about this," she said.

"Just because you wish you had brothers and sisters doesn't mean I do," he told her gently.

"Deny, deny," she retorted. "You'll realize it eventually."

"My darling analyst/assistant, stop thinking about me, and focus on yourself."

The car entered the palace gates and stopped outside the side door of the palace.

Sophie drew in a quick breath. "I think we're here."

"Yeah, I guess we are," Max said. "I think I should go inside with you."

Surprise rushed through Sophie. "Why? Do you really think they're going to mistreat me?"

Max frowned. "No, but—"

"Didn't you say I needed to start relaxing?" she asked, wishing she didn't feel like she needed a nap.

"I guess so," he muttered.

"Then that's what I plan to do," she said and accepted the driver's hand as he helped her from the car.

"I'll walk you in," he said.

"Not necessary," she said and shut the car door.

Sophie awakened in the middle of the night and took a potty break. She returned to her bed, but a female staff member was waiting.

"Can I help you with anything, Miss Taylor?"

Startled, she nodded. "I'm fine, thank you."

"Very well. If you need anything, please call," the woman said.

Sophie nodded and climbed into bed. She didn't know if she would ever adjust to palace staff. So far, they both surprised and alarmed her. Taking a deep breath, she closed her eyes. She needed to rest so she could get back to her own apartment.

She awakened the next morning, or afternoon… Sophie wasn't sure which. Squinting her eyes, she glanced at her clock. Ten o'clock in the morning. How embarrassing. She couldn't recall when she'd slept this late when it wasn't due to a time-zone change.

She dragged herself out of bed and into the shower. Standing in the spray, she absorbed the comfort and invigoration of the water. After several moments, she stepped out of the shower and rubbed a towel over herself.

Pulling on a robe, she walked into her bedroom and found Pippa waiting for her at a small breakfast table. "Good morning," the princess with the wild, wiry hair said. "I have a semi-American breakfast for you. Coffee, tea, eggs, prosciutto, croissants and marmalade. Does that sound good?"

"Perfect," Sophie said as she joined Pippa at the table. "It's perfect. How did you know?"

"I have an American husband," Pippa said, lifting her cup of tea. "He considers our breakfasts quite wimpy. He requires meat or eggs. Or both. I swear, the man would eat steak for breakfast."

Sophie laughed. "Steak and eggs is a popular breakfast combo in the States, but I have to tell you that I've never eaten steak in the morning."

"So, it's not all that usual?" Pippa asked. "Nic acts as if it's an everyday occurrence for everyone."

"He's definitely pulling your leg," Sophie said and took a bite of scrambled eggs.

"Pulling my leg?" Pippa repeated, clearly confused.

"Fooling you," Sophie said.

Pippa frowned. "Is that so? Then I shall give him something horrid for breakfast. What do you suggest?"

Sophie shrugged. "I don't know. Liver?"

Pippa's mouth lifted from a frown to a smile. "Excellent. Liver. Is there anything worse to your American taste?"

Sophie searched her culinary memory. "Um, chitlins?"

"What's that?" Pippa asked.

"Look it up on Google."

Pippa nodded while she clicked away on her cell phone's keyboard. "That bad," she said with a smile.

"Let's change conversation. How are you feeling this morning?"

"Better," Sophie said and took another bite of eggs followed by toast.

"Dizzy at all?" Pippa asked, and took a bite of a crumpet.

"No, thank goodness," Sophie said.

Pippa nodded. "That's wonderful news. But we would be happy for you to stay here an extra night."

Sophie shook her head. "Not necessary."

Pippa sighed. "We're always glad to have someone new and interesting at the palace. Are you sure you can't stay?"

"I may be new, but I'm not sure about interesting. Thanks for the invite, though. How are you feeling?" she asked, glancing at Pippa's pregnant belly.

"Excited," Pippa said, then frowned. "And uncomfortable. I've been told the baby has dropped. There's no comfortable position."

"Sorry," Sophie said. "How far along are you?"

"Thirty eight weeks and two days," she said.

Sophie wondered if she was also recording the hours and minutes. "Hopefully, it won't be much longer."

"Hopefully," Pippa said and sighed. "But it's all a matter of perspective. We lost Nic's mother to terminal cancer last year. She was ready to go, but we weren't ready for her to leave. We miss her so much."

Sophie's heart clenched. "That must have been hard."

Pippa nodded. "It was. But we're naming our baby after her. Amelie was pure magic." Pippa smiled. "During those last months, she would scare us to death by escaping the cottage and going to the beach on her own."

"It's wonderful that you're naming the baby after Nic's mother," Sophie said. "That's so—loving."

Pippa lifted her cup and nodded. "I wish you had met Amelie. She was a wonderful combination of boldness, wisdom and fun. In the short time I knew her, I learned a lot. The biggest lesson was don't waste your life. Go for it. Life is short and love is the most important gift of all. If you love someone, then you've got to give the chance to be with them all you've got."

Sophie took a sip of coffee and tried not to squirm. Did she really *love* Max? Or did she just have an intense crush on him? Setting her cup down, she stared into the warm brown liquid, wishing it could offer her answers. If she gave in to her feelings, would she have the nerve to go after him? What if she made a fool of herself? What if he completely rejected her?

Her stomach twisted and clenched.

"Are you okay?" Pippa asked, concern etched across her face. "You look a bit ill."

"No. I'm fine. Just need more coffee," Sophie said.

"Well, I'm certain you could use more than coffee. I can tell you're probably one of those types who wouldn't complain even if you had a broken leg, but your body has been through a traumatic experience. Getting hit by that motor scooter," Pippa said, shaking her head. "I think I'd want to hide under the covers for a few days to catch my breath. It's a miracle you weren't hurt worse. You could have been—" She broke off as if she realized she should be more encouraging. "But you weren't. You're fine and you're just going to get better and better."

Sophie nodded in agreement, but her brain was stuck on what Pippa hadn't said. She could have been *killed.* Her brain instantly went into denial. *Killed?* That was a little overdramatic, wasn't it? Her injuries could have been much more serious, but to think that she could have died... Frowning, Sophie firmly shoved the possibility to the back of her mind. A dark place she did her best not to visit.

"Oh, my," Pippa said, putting her hand on her belly and smiling. "Amelie has hiccups." She laughed. "Would you like to feel it?"

Sophie had wondered what it would feel like to have a baby inside her. To feel it move. "Sure," she said and stood next to Pippa, who guided Sophie's hand to her belly.

Sophie felt the rhythmic bump inside Pippa. "Oh, poor thing," she said.

"She actually gets them pretty often. It makes me wonder if I'm eating something that bothers her. Sorry, Amelie," she said and rubbed her belly.

At that moment, a strange awareness sliced through Sophie. She'd avoided the very idea of having a baby. She'd avoided the very idea of being loved by Max, although she'd secretly wished for it.

She felt Pippa's gaze on her and tried to shake off her thoughts.

"Are you okay?" Pippa asked, reaching toward her.

"Fine," Sophie said. "Just a little dazed."

"From the accident?" Pippa asked. "Perhaps you should spend another night here at the palace."

Sophie shook her head. "I'm just a little behind on my coffee. I'll be ready for anything in a few minutes."

"If you say so," Pippa said doubtfully.

"I do," Sophie said and patted Pippa's hand. "And thank you for being so caring."

Pippa insisted that Sophie stay at the palace through the early afternoon. Sophie left as soon as she could, arriving at her apartment and pacing. Could she have died? Was she being overdramatic?

She shook her head from side to side. Truth was that not everyone survived being smacked by a scooter. She could have been paralyzed or worse.

Sophie thought of herself as being stronger than that, though. She was strong enough to overcome this. A little brush with a scooter couldn't knock her out forever. She'd survived challenges in every country she'd visited. She was a mule.

Max had even referred to her in that manner, and she hadn't been insulted or disagreed. She was strong, resilient. She could make it through anything. Right? She put her doubts from her mind and watched a television show.

Dinnertime arrived and her cell phone rang. It was Max.

"How are you feeling?"

"Much better. I left the palace a couple hours ago."

"What can I bring you for dinner?"

Surprised by his offer, she automatically refused.

"You don't need to bring anything. I can pull a box of something from the freezer."

"I think you could use something better than that. I'll be over in an hour or so," he said and hung up.

"But—" she said and sighed. The truth was she wasn't hungry. She hadn't been hungry since the accident. If she told Max that, though, he would think she had been terminally injured.

Sophie puttered around her apartment for awhile then sat down on the couch. She leaned her head back for just a few minutes....

The doorbell jolted her from her sleep. Her heart hammered against her chest and she jumped to her feet. Taking a quick breath, she rushed to the door and opened it.

Max stood in front of her holding two bags, two bottles of beer and a bottle of wine. She blinked. "Wow. What's all this?"

"Steak, baked potato, salad. Took forever for me to find this in take-out," he said. "And I'm betting the steak is nowhere as good as we got in Australia."

"Probably," she said, taking a bag, wondering how she could possibly eat half the meal he had brought for her.

"But the reviewers said this place made the best steak in Chantaine," he said.

She took the food from the bag and placed it on the table. Glancing at the steak, she shook her head. "Max, this steak is the size of Gibraltar."

"Well, maybe you can eat some for leftovers tomorrow," he said.

"Tomorrow," she muttered. "Try the whole week."

"You've got to get your strength back. This will help," he insisted. "Have a seat. Do you want beer or wine?"

"Water, just in case I take a pain pill when I go to bed tonight," she said.

"You're still hurting?" he asked, worry creasing his face.

"I'm fine. I'm going to be fine. I'm lucky that scooter threw me clear," she reassured him. She was flattered by his attention. She'd wanted to feel him focus on her, but she was cautious to take it to heart. "What are you so worried about me for?"

"You didn't see yourself hooked up to all those tubes," he said. "Sit down and eat."

His expression made her stomach tighten. "I know I was knocked out, but it wasn't that bad. Was it?"

Max met her gaze. "You're the strongest woman I've ever met. It was hard to see you in that condition."

She cut a bite of her steak. "Well, I'm not in that condition now."

"Thank God," he muttered and lifted a bite to his mouth.

She also chewed a bite of steak and looked at Max. "Why were you so alarmed? In the scheme of things, I'm just an employee. I'm technically replaceable."

He looked at her as if she were crazy. "You must think I'm a nut job," he said. "You're not replaceable. I learned that a long time ago."

She watched him carefully as she took another bite of her meal. "My mom said you sounded upset when you called her. She was afraid she would need to make funeral arrangements."

"I probably overreacted. I'd never seen you anywhere near that condition," he said, continuing to eat. "I even called my own mother."

Sophie blinked. "Your own mother? Why in the world would you call her?"

"I've told her about you. She would want to know."

Sophie stared at him. She didn't know what to think. "Well, I'm glad I didn't croak. It would have been terribly inconvenient given that I'm here in Chantaine."

"Yeah," Max said and glanced at her plate. "Stop talking and eat."

Sophie looked at her plate and the steak seemed to have increased in size. Sighing, she took another bite. She watched Max down both beers as he consumed his meal.

"So what did you think of the palace?" he asked.

"It was very nice. The room was a little smaller than I expected, but I guess since the building is so old, that should be expected. Princess Pippa was so sweet. Being with them made me wish I had a sister, but I guess it's a little too late to wish for that," Sophie said.

"Really?" Max said, leaning back in his seat. "I can't imagine wanting sisters."

She scowled at him. "That's because you have them," she said.

"I didn't know that until recently. Now it feels like I'm supposed to be a big brother family guy," he said.

"There are worse things," she said, sipping her water.

He glanced at her plate. "You didn't eat half your meal."

"I'm not hungry. You sound like a big brother," she said. "Is that how you feel toward me? Brotherly?"

He met her eyes, clearly uncomfortable. "Not brotherly. Protective," he said. "You and I have worked together for years. I don't want anything to happen to you."

Sophie laughed then took another sip of water. "Oh, my goodness. I'm starting to feel important."

Max rolled his eyes. "Don't go over the edge. And you're still not eating."

"I told you, I'm not hungry," she grunted.

He frowned. "That's not good."

"It's normal," she said. "The nurse told me I might not have a big appetite."

"You need to build up your strength."

"Gradually," she said and stood, feeling tired. "I think I want to go to bed early."

"Maybe I should stay," he said.

She shook her head. "Not necessary."

He knocked back the last of his beer. "I don't agree."

She scowled at him. "I'm really okay."

"That's debatable," he said. "So, I'll take the sofa. Are you sure you won't eat more?"

"I'm not hungry," she said in a low voice. "But thank you."

"Okay, I'll wrap it up," he said.

"I can do it."

"No," he said. "You get ready to hit the sack."

Sophie sighed. "Thanks for coming by tonight."

"I wouldn't have considered anything else," he said.

It was a totally different experience having Max hover over her. Although they often shared close work quarters, she'd had to learn to dismiss her physical attraction to him or she would never get any work done. She hadn't been perfect at the game, though. Max possessed a tall, muscular physique. His physical strength was a tremendous turn-on. But there was no work to be done, at least not for now.

She turned toward her small bedroom then whirled as she remembered she should at least offer him a pillow and a blanket. She walked straight into his chest. "Oops," she said, her heart racing against her rib cage.

He caught her arms with his hands. "Problem?"

She read the concern on his face again and took a deep breath. "No. I just wanted to get you a pillow and blanket."

He shrugged. "It's no big deal. You know I've slept on the ground in a lot of places."

She inhaled his masculine scent and tried not to get drunk from it. "That's not necessary tonight. I'll be right back," she said, but it took a few extra seconds for her to pull away. Finally managing to detach herself, she headed down the hall and gathered the blanket, pillow and an extra set of sheets that wouldn't fit the sofa, but would definitely feel better against Max's skin. She grabbed a few toiletries, too.

"Here's a toothbrush, some soap and some linens. If you need anything else, let me know," she said as she set the items on the coffee table.

"This is way more than I need," he protested, raking his hand through his hair.

"No worries," she said, using the vernacular from Australia. "I'll let you get your own water glass in the cupboard."

She met his gaze for a quick moment and her heart dipped. "There you go. That's my Sophie coming back. Go get some rest. You'll be your regular dose of piss and vinegar tomorrow."

"That's not the most flattering description," she told him then turned away and headed for her bedroom. It was clear that Max would never see her as a woman.

Chapter Four

Sophie tossed and turned for a good hour before drifting restlessly to sleep. She dreamed a dozen crazy dreams involving a scooter, the hospital, Max and the palace. She awakened at 3:00 a.m., her mouth as dry as the desert.

Pushing back her covers, she climbed out of her bed and headed for the small galley kitchen to get a glass of water. She should have planned for this, but she'd been too addled by Max's presence. Moving as quietly as possible, she opened a kitchen cabinet.

From behind her, she heard his voice. "You okay?"

Sophie nearly jumped out of her skin. "I'm fine. I didn't mean to wake you."

"I sleep lightly sometimes," he said. "You want some water?"

"Yes," she said and turned as he pulled a glass from the cabinet. She felt his body pressed against hers. It took her breath.

A half beat later, he moved away. She wished he'd stay and go at the same time. He filled the glass with water from the spigot and offered it to her.

"Thanks," she said and gulped down half of it.

"How are you feeling?" he asked.

"Okay. Just a little sore. I didn't take any pain meds tonight."

"Mistake?"

"Maybe," she said. "I feel a little achy. I'm sure I'll be better in the morning."

"Don't plan on coming to work tomorrow," he said.

"I'll be bored," she complained.

"You need another day or two," he said and lifted his hand to slide his fingers through her hair.

She stood stock still at his touch. It felt so good. A little moan escaped her lips. She immediately felt self-conscious.

"Feels good?" he asked and continued to stroke her scalp.

"Yes," she whispered and closed her eyes.

He continued to stroke and she couldn't hold back another moan.

"That sound," he muttered. "It's so—" He broke off and she felt his face lower closer to hers.

Her heart hammered against her chest so hard she could barely breathe.

"Dammit, Sophie," he said and pressed his mouth against hers.

It was the sweetest, most powerful and sensual sensation she'd ever experienced. She opened her lips and his tongue slid inside her mouth. So sexy. She savored every second. A few breaths later he pulled back.

"Damn. I shouldn't have done that," he said quietly.

Her heart contracted. Her emotions shattered in a thousand pieces. She tried to pull herself back together. Several breaths later, she nodded, though inside she was shaking her head. "You're right. You shouldn't have."

With trembling hands, she grabbed her glass of water and skittered away from the kitchen. She'd just had the best and worst experience of her life. How could she possibly go to sleep? How could she possibly face Max in the morning?

Although it felt like hours later, Sophie eventually fell asleep. She awakened to a fresh glass of water on her nightstand and a note. *Sleep in. Need you back healthy and whole. Take another day. —Max*

Frowning at the note, she rose and took a long swig of her water. How convenient for him to leave. Now, she had to wonder if she would feel uncomfortable when she saw him again. Her head and body ached. She should have taken some pain killer, but she didn't like putting foreign substances into her body.

Swearing under her breath, she walked into the shower and prayed it would help her aching body. After several minutes of standing under the spray, Sophie dried off and returned to sit on her bed, her brain spinning.

How much had she screwed up by responding to Max's kiss? He had started it, but damn, she had been ready, wanting and willing. She supposed she should have resisted, but couldn't imagine trying. Sophie had been waiting for *years* for Max to see her as someone other than his assistant. When he'd kissed her, half her dreams had come true. Then those dreams had been demolished.

In his mind, he had given in to a momentary lapse. In her mind, this was the big moment she had been waiting for.

Two completely opposite reactions.

She had wanted to feel his strong chest against hers. She had yearned for his arms to wrap around her and pull her to him.

But he had kissed her then regretted it within seconds. Regretted it so much that he stopped mid-kiss.

The knowledge tore at her. How could Sophie possibly return to work with Max knowing that he didn't want her and never would? She'd learned that in the middle of the night.

Did he know that she wanted him? Could he tell? Had she successfully faked her agreement with him? Her stomach twisted. She hated that she *had* to fake it.

Desperation grabbed at her. Unable to sit still, she rose from the bed and paced around the small apartment. Sophie hated feeling desperate. She'd always worked hard to avoid the feeling. She much preferred being in control and had learned from a young age to use her willpower to keep her from feeling vulnerable. Since her father had abandoned her mother and her soon after Sophie had been born, she'd sensed her mother's desperation. Every once in a while when one of his sporadic checks came in the mail, she could feel her mother's stress level ease up, but it never seemed to last.

Until last year. It was as if her mother had finally realized that Sophie would be able to take care of herself and she didn't need to worry and fret about the future quite so much. This past holiday had been the best time she'd shared with her mother in years. Her mother had laughed more, and so had Sophie even though she'd been distracted wondering how Max's visit with the Devereauxes had gone.

Impatience nicked at her. A twinge of anger followed. Why should she feel desperate? She'd survived the scooter accident. She'd survived a snake bite just a few months ago when they were in Australia. There was no reason for her to feel so vulnerable. Yet, she did.

Sophie scowled at the knowledge. She needed to fix this. She needed to do something that made her feel less vulnerable. Today. She put on jogging clothes, exited her apartment complex and began to run. She triple-checked herself and everyone else at street-crossings then headed up into the hills of Chantaine. It was a beautiful island and her goal was to find a fantastic view. Sophie was a sucker for a beautiful sight.

Climbing a long hill, Sophie finally reached the summit and caught her breath as she looked over the island. The green foliage and rocky shore contrasted against the deep-blue ocean. She wasn't sure she could live on Chantaine forever, but she could certainly live here for awhile.

Breathing in the ocean air, she savored the view. Life was fragile. She could have lost hers just a few days ago. She needed to make choices. Sophie had a decent savings in her bank. Maybe she needed to start thinking less about security and more about what she wanted in her life for the long-term.

Sophie rested at the crest of the hill for awhile then returned to the city, again triple-checking the crosswalks. Stumbling into her apartment, she gulped down her water and slumped in a chair.

Her cell phone rang. Sophie glanced at the caller ID. Phillipa. "Hi, your highness. How are you?"

"I'm fine," Pippa said. "But Eve is in labor. I'm so excited I can't stand it."

Sophie noticed that Pippa sounded out of breath. "Are you okay?"

"Yes, just excited," Pippa said.

"Are you having contractions?"

A long silence followed. "I don't think so," she said tentatively.

"Where are you?" Sophie asked.

"At the palace," Pippa said. "I'm taking care of Stephenia, Stefan and Eve's daughter."

"Pippa, you don't sound so good. Maybe you should go to the hospital," Sophie said.

"I'm fine," Pippa said brightly. "Oops. I need to go. Stephenia is tearing up the toy room."

Sophie frowned. She had an uncomfortable feeling

about Pippa. Taking a quick shower, she dressed and paced. She called Pippa and waited. It went to voice mail.

Moments later, Sophie's phone rang. "You were right," Pippa said. "I'm having contractions. Nic is going to be so peeved if he doesn't get here in time."

"How can I help?" Sophie asked.

"If it's not too much trouble, could you come to the hospital? I'm afraid Bridget would make me more nervous."

"I'll be there as soon as I can," Sophie said. "I'm honored you would ask me."

"You may not be honored when I start screaming," Pippa said. "I'm all for pain relief."

Sophie laughed and hung up. It took just a few moments for her to get to the hospital. Surprisingly enough, she was led into Pippa's private birthing unit. Surrounded by nurses, Pippa met Sophie's gaze. Pippa looked as if she were drowning.

"Hurts," Pippa said.

Sophie rushed to her side. "Then take the pain meds."

"I feel guilty."

"That's wrong," Sophie said, thinking back to when she refused to take her own pain meds. "This will be hard on your body. No need to suffer more than usual."

"But I don't want to hurt the baby," Pippa said.

"Then listen to your nurses," Sophie said. "They see this every day."

Soon enough, Pippa allowed herself to be anesthetized. She took a deep breath. "This is so much better. When you have a baby, you should get an epidural."

"I'll remember that," Sophie promised.

"I hope Nic gets here," Pippa said.

Princess Pippa's wish came true. Less than an hour later, Nic arrived from a transatlantic flight. Rushed and worried, he made his way to Pippa's side. Sophie squeezed Pippa's hand then dismissed herself. All was right. Husband was with his pregnant wife. Life was as it should be. She gave her cell phone number to the nurse on duty.

Sophie returned to her apartment, but wasn't inclined to stay inside. She walked around her neighborhood and bought bunches of flowers for both Pippa and Eve in anticipation of their babies. She dumped them in water and turned on the television in her apartment, halfway watching, more so listening for her cell phone.

Hours later, it finally rang. "Miss Sophie Taylor," a female voice said.

"Yes," Sophie said, rising to a sitting position.

"Her Highness Princess Pippa requested that I call you to tell you that she has delivered a beautiful daughter named Amelie."

Sophie felt a rush of relief. "I'm so happy. Please tell her thank you for me, along with my congratulations."

"I will, ma'am," the woman said.

Seconds later, her phone buzzed again. Sophie picked up. "Yes," she said.

"Miss Sophie Taylor," the man said.

"Yes," she said. "This is about Stefan and Eve's baby, isn't it? Please tell me she's okay."

"Yes, Her Highness is quite well. The baby boy is also quite fine. Princess Eve asked me to convey the news."

"Thank you." Sophie said. "I'm thrilled for everyone."

Seconds later, her cell phone rang again. The incoming call was from Max.

She picked up. "Yes?"

"What's with all these royal babies tonight?" he asked in a gruff voice.

"Welcome to being an uncle," she said. "I'm going to the hospital."

"Now?" he asked.

She scowled at him even though he couldn't see her. "Now," she said and hung up her phone.

Without thinking, Sophie grabbed the flowers and a cab then went to the hospital. She sent the flowers up to both Eve and Pippa, hoping they would make it to the intended recipients.

She paced the hospital waiting room for a few moments wondering why exactly she had come to the hospital for the second time, then decided to leave. Heading out the hospital door, she walked smack into Max. He caught her by her arms.

"Hey. What are you doing here?"

"I brought flowers, but I think they're probably too busy to notice, so I decided to leave."

He shoved his hands into his pockets. "That was nice of you."

"It seemed the right thing to do," she said.

"Maybe I should get a toy for them or something," he said.

"I'm sure they would be happy with your good wishes," she said and shrugged.

"I guess this means we don't get to see the newborns," he said.

"We can look forward to seeing photos online and in the newspaper," she said and smiled. "Uncle Max."

He scowled at her. "So why did I come to the hospital?" he asked.

"Because you care more than you admit," she said, relieved that he hadn't brought up the kiss they'd shared. Maybe they could just go back to the way things had been before, she thought hopefully.

He scowled again. "I'm leaving."

"Me, too," she said and followed him outside the door.

"You want a drink?" he asked.

"It's been an interesting day," she said, remembering those hours she'd spent trying to comfort Pippa. "I think I'll take you up on it."

"I'll get a cab."

Soon enough, they sat in an American-style bar. A waiter quickly served them. Beer for both of them. He lifted his glass and she clinked hers against his. "Cheers," she said. "Uncle Max times two."

He shot her a dark look. "Cheers," he said and drank his beer.

Sophie sipped hers. "Pippa was impressive. I didn't see Eve, but I'm sure she did quite well. Pippa didn't even realize she was in labor at first."

"How can that be?" Max asked. "How can a woman not know she's in labor?"

"I don't know," Sophie said. "But Pippa didn't. I'm glad her husband showed up."

"Was she screaming when you were with her?" he asked.

"No," Sophie said. "She was uncomfortable, but focused."

"I've heard labor is like a kidney stone," Max said, taking another gulp of beer.

"I wouldn't know because I've had neither a baby nor a kidney stone," she teased.

"Yeah, well, you're the perfect girl. No mistakes," he said and took another swig.

Sophie frowned. "What is that supposed to mean?"

He shrugged his broad shoulders. "Nothing. Really." He paused. "Just that some people get their stuff together faster than others."

"I'm not sure how to take that," Sophie said. "I've always felt I needed to have my *stuff* together. There was no backup plan for me."

"Yeah, I know that," Max said. "Other people with no backup plan don't do nearly as well as you do."

"You haven't done too poorly yourself," she said, lifting her beer mug to him.

"Maybe," he said and took another long swig of beer. "Maybe."

A flash of the memory of Max's mouth against hers slid through Sophie's mind. Her body immediately responded. Heat scored through her. She took a long gulp of beer even though she didn't like it much. She prayed it would cool her off, inside and out.

"This royal stuff sucks," Max murmured.

"It could be worse," Sophie said. "What if you were the father-to-be?" she asked.

"Never gonna happen," he said. "I'm too careful."

"Hmm," she said.

"What does that mean?"

"Never could be a long time," she said. "You're pretty good with kids considering you're saying you'll never have any."

"Between my genes and upbringing, I don't think I'm cut out for getting myself in a family way."

"Maybe you're right," she said. Sophie was growing tired of trying to prove to Max that he could fall in love and it would be okay. She still believed he could fall in love, but more than ever, she was starting to believe that she wasn't the woman who could make him fall.

The next morning, Sophie returned to work. Even though things between them had been easy last night, she was still nervous. She hoped she wouldn't feel awkward or get distracted by her attraction to him.

As he placed a mug of coffee on her desk, she noticed his hand, that same strong hand that had held her against him. She couldn't stop herself from lifting her gaze to his face, his lips, his eyes. Darn, she thought. He was clearly fine and had wiped the memory of kissing her from his mind. Must be nice, she thought with a frown.

"G'mornin'," he said in his sexy rumble.

She barely resisted scowling. "Good morning," she said. "How are you?"

"The question is how are *you?*" he asked.

"Fine, thank you. Ready to get to work," she said.

"Okay," he said and went to his desk. He picked up the Nerf ball they often tossed between each other when they were discussing a problem. "Bad news. I just lost one of my backhoe operators. And the back hoe itself is broken." He tossed her the Nerf ball.

She caught it. "Well, you need another backhoe. We can take care of that easily enough with your influence. And in terms of the backhoe operator, maybe I could learn."

Max frowned at her and lifted his hands for her to send him the Nerf ball. She tossed it.

"You're recovering from a concussion and—"

"I'm recovered," she interrupted.

"You don't have the ball," Max said.

She scowled at him.

"You're recovering from a concussion. I don't want you putting yourself at risk," he said.

She waved her fingers at herself for him to send her the Nerf ball. He did, although she could tell it was tossed reluctantly. "I've *never* had an automobile accident. I highly doubt I would have a backhoe accident. You need to remember that the scooter ran into me at a stoplight. *I* was not at fault."

He gave her the sign for her to send the ball to him. She did, reluctantly.

"It doesn't matter that you weren't at fault. You were hurt. I'm not willing to risk that again."

She was torn between his protectiveness and his

crankiness. She lifted her hands and caught the ball. "If I were a guy, you wouldn't be acting like this," she said.

He met her gaze for a long moment.

The door to the trailer burst open and Terri strode inside. "I hear you need a backhoe operator. I can drive any piece of construction equipment you give me. And my husband, Bob, is loving the beach."

Sophie couldn't help smiling at Terri's arrival. She rose and flew toward the woman to give her a big hug.

Terri hugged her back. "How's everything?"

"Same as always," Sophie said brightly.

Terri rolled her eyes. "Well, dang," she said. "Maybe we can do something about…"

"Not everything is same as always," Max said. "Sophie was in a bad accident last week and was hospitalized."

"What?" Terri asked, her eyes growing wide with concern.

"I'm fine," Sophie said.

"So she says," Max said.

"I am fine," Sophie insisted.

Terri looked from Max to Sophie. "Okeydoke. Whatever you say. I'm here for the backhoe job." She shot Sophie a sideways glance.

Sophie took a deep breath. She didn't like where this was headed. She was happy to see Terri, but suspected the woman would start giving her advice about romance. Sophie was also feeling a bit claustrophobic being in the same trailer with Max. She was way too aware of his every move. She was going to have to figure out a way around this. "Welcome back," she said to Terri then turned to Max. "Just so you know, I plan on leaving by 6:00 p.m. for the next couple of days."

He nodded. "Good. I want you to take care of yourself. Leave earlier if that's what you need."

Sophie set her cell phone alarm for 6:00 p.m. and forced herself to rise from her desk chair. In the past, she would have stayed late into the evening because she loved being around Max. After that blasted kiss, she was feeling too aware of him. What made it worse was he'd clearly dismissed the incident with no problem at all.

Sophie dashed from the trailer and took a deep breath. As soon as she slid into her car, she felt a sliver of relief. The tension she felt from sharing the same space with him eased. Thank goodness. Sophie took another few breaths and started the car.

Arriving home too early to her apartment, she flittered and fluttered throughout the small space. Her cell phone rang and she picked up.

"Miss Sophie Taylor, this is Senior Aide Giorno from the Devereaux palace. You are invited to a reception celebrating the birth of His Royal Highness Prince Stefan and Princess Eve's new child and the child of Her Highness Princess Phillipa and her husband, Nic Lafitte."

"Wonderful. Name the date," she said.

"Saturday at three o'clock," the palace aide said.

"Thank you very much. I'll be there," Sophie said.

"Very well. We look forward to your presence," the palace rep said. "Good evening."

Sophie took a long draw from her glass of water. Good for her. She'd taken care of Saturday. She only needed to avoid Max for three more days.

Chapter Five

Finally, Saturday arrived.

Sophie couldn't remember a time in her life when three days had seemed to pass so slowly. Friday night had been the toughest. She would be the last to admit it, but by 6:00 p.m. on Wednesday and Thursday she'd been tired. A small meal and a little boring television and she'd been more than ready for sleep. On Friday evening, however, she was jittery. And bored. Television sucked. She ended up trying to do some work on her laptop, but thoughts of Max relentlessly crept into her thoughts. Finally her mind gave up and when she awakened on Saturday, she was ready for an outing. She was very excited at the prospect of seeing the new babies and honored that she'd been asked to attend.

Sophie took a taxi to the palace and was immediately

escorted to a ballroom. She heard babies crying as she entered. "Good lungs," she said.

The escort chuckled. "Excellent attitude."

A huge line formed to meet the new royal babies. Sophie hated the idea of being one more person to add to the marathon of greetings the royal couples faced, but like everyone else in line, she couldn't wait to see the new babies. After she'd stood in line several moments, she felt a nudge. She glanced up to Max's face.

"Mind if I join you?" he asked.

"You're butting," she said bluntly.

"Give me a break. I can't imagine waiting in a mile-long line to meet a screaming baby," he said.

"Then why are you here?"

He shrugged. "Seemed the right thing to do."

She met his gaze. "You're such a faker," she said.

His eyes widened. "What?"

"You want to see those babies. You can deny it all you want, but you do," she said. "You actually *like* babies. You actually *like* your new relatives."

He narrowed his eyes at her. "Okay, I like them, but that's all."

"Hmm," she said and turned away from him.

A few seconds of silence passed. "So, what have you been doing after six o'clock?" he asked.

"Enjoying life," she said.

"You haven't been bored out of your mind?" he asked.

"Of course not," she lied.

She was saved from a cross-examination when a woman approached them. "Miss Sophie Taylor and Mr.

Maxwell Carter. You've been requested to come to the front of the receiving line."

Max muttered under his breath. Sophie elbowed him. They were led first to Pippa holding her baby as she stood with her husband.

Sophie gave a quick curtsey.

"Stop that," Pippa said. "You helped me while I was in labor. This my husband, Nic Lafitte."

"Pleased to meet you, Mr. Lafitte," Sophie said. "Amelie is beautiful."

Max frowned at her. "How do you know the baby's name?"

"Pippa and I chatted the night I stayed at the palace," Sophie said and smiled at the baby, who was sleeping. "So precious."

"Yes. She is," Nic Lafitte said. "Thank you for helping my wife until I arrived."

"My pleasure," Sophie said.

"And it's good to see the newest member of the De-vereauxes again," Nic said.

"My last name is Carter," Max said grudgingly.

Nic nodded. "Good to see you again, Max Carter. I hear you're doing some good work on the roads on the north end of the island. I hope to take advantage of the improvements once they're complete."

"It will be much nicer for both the people who live there and for visitors. I had toyed with working on the alternate dirt road that some of the locals use, but I don't think we'll have time."

As Nic and Max continued their discussion about road

construction, Pippa leaned toward Sophie. "Watch out for Bridget," she whispered.

"Why?" Sophie asked.

"She's got an idea for you."

"Me?" Sophie asked, feeling an odd mix of caution and curiosity. "I can't imagine…"

"You don't have to imagine. Bridget will do it for you," Pippa warned. "Good luck."

Seconds later the aide led Sophie and Max to the front of the long line to meet Stefan and Eve's baby. Their baby boy was screaming at the top of his lungs.

Sophie smiled. "He's gorgeous."

"Healthy," Max said.

Stefan grimaced. "You are both too polite. Our son has colic," he said.

"Poor guy has a constant tummy ache," Eve said, looking worn out.

"You're due a break after your challenging pregnancy," Sophie said. "Make sure you call in your nanny so you can rest."

"Thank you," Stefan agreed. "Eve needs her rest."

"But he is beautiful," Sophie said of the red-faced, screaming baby. "I bet he will be a delight in three months or less."

"We can only hope." Eve leaned toward Sophie. "Pippa's baby is so mild."

"You and Stefan have strong personalities. Did you expect anything different?" Sophie asked.

Eve shot her a tired smile. "Good point."

Sophie hesitated for a second then shrugged off her

wariness. "You've probably tried all the usual tricks, but would you mind if I held him for a moment?"

Both Stefan and Eve looked at her in surprise. It was clear that Eve was suffering from a new mother's desperation. She nodded and gingerly handed her baby to Sophie. "Of course, if you can help him…"

Sophie held the small, warm little baby against her and walked a few steps away while Max chatted with Stefan and Eve. His body was stiff with discomfort. "All those gas bubbles hurt," she murmured and began to massage the baby's back. "So much easier back in the old days getting your food from Mom in the womb. You didn't have to work for it then, did you, sweetie?" she said as she continued to massage his back.

Stefan Jr. let out a gigantic burp, then another. "There you go," she praised him. "I bet you'll be much happier now." She returned the relaxed infant to Eve.

"A back massage?" Eve said in disbelief. "I would have never thought of that."

Sophie nodded. "I babysat infants a lot when I was in high school and early college. If you think about it, it makes sense. A back massage makes adults feel good too. And of course, now that the air is gone, he'll probably want to feed again."

"Well, thank you for the tip. I hope we can repeat it when necessary," Eve said.

Sophie smiled and felt a whirl of motion beside her. "Bridget," she said as soon as she recognized the princess. She began to curtsey and Bridget waved the gesture aside.

"Not necessary." She waved at Max. "Please let me borrow your lovely Sophie," she said and drew Sophie away. "I have a favor to ask. There's a special dinner honoring our historical awareness and we're a little light on special guests. I was hoping you could join us."

Sophie blinked then cleared her throat. "That's very nice, but I wouldn't call myself special."

"Oh, but you are," Bridget said. "We love Americans. Please say yes."

"Uh, I guess," Sophie said warily.

"Perfect," Bridget said. "And I've already arranged an escort for you—"

"Escort?" Sophie echoed.

"He's lovely. One of Stefan's economic advisors. David Rinaldo."

"An economic advisor," Sophie repeated.

"I know it sounds boring, but he's part Italian, so he can't be all bad. Italian men are the best," Bridget said.

"Then why did you marry an American?" Sophie asked.

Bridget rolled her eyes. "Totally unplanned, but it was fate."

Seconds later two young boys scrambled through the crowd and latched themselves on to Bridget's legs. "Well, hello, my darlings. How did you get loose from your father?"

"Mama," one of the boys said.

"Cookie?" the other asked hopefully.

"Excuse me," she said to Sophie and smiled at the boys, gently stroking their hair back from their fore-heads. "I definitely think you should have a cookie, but you must let go of my legs or I can't walk to the table to get them for you."

The twins immediately released their death grip on Bridget's legs. She glanced at Sophie. "Boys, I'd like you to say hello to Miss Sophie."

"Hello, Mizz Sophie," they chorused, though Sophie could tell that they were preoccupied with the idea of a cookie.

Sophie bent down and shook each of their hands. "So nice to meet you both." Then she stood and met Bridget's gaze. "I think you have a promise to keep."

"Of course I do," she said and extended her hands to the young twins. "Come along now. I'll be in touch," she said over her shoulder. "So will David Rinaldo. Don't forget the name."

"Who's David Rinaldo?" Max asked from behind her.

Sophie felt her face heat with self-consciousness. "One of Stefan's economic advisors. I don't know much about him. The boys were determined to get cookies."

Max lifted his eyebrows. "Are there cookies?"

Sophie resisted the urge to roll her eyes. The same distraction technique that worked on toddler boys worked on a thirty-year-old male? "That's what I hear," she said. "Maybe at that table. There seems to be a crowd."

Max caught her hand, taking her by surprise. "Let's go. Everyone feels happier after they eat a cookie."

The following day, Sophie received a call from David Rinaldo asking her to meet him for a drink after work. "I must go," she told Max as she shut down her laptop.

"I was thinking we would review the day and make plans for tomorrow," he said.

"Not me," she said. "I have plans."

"What plans?"

She shrugged. "Just plans. I'll see you tomorrow. Ciao."

"Ciao," he called after her. "What's with *ciao?*"

"It's just a friendly greeting. There's no need to get worked up over it," she said.

He frowned at her for a long moment. "Are you meeting a man tonight?"

She lifted her hands. "What if I am? You don't care about my personal life, do you?"

His frown deepened. "Not unless it interferes with your work."

"It won't. I shouldn't be staying past 6:00 p.m. anyway. Right?"

Max hesitated then nodded. "Yeah," he said reluctantly. "Right."

"Have a good night," she said and stepped outside the door before he could reply. *Sheesh,* Max could turn into the grilling kind. That wouldn't be fun. She tried to shake off his inquisition then took a deep breath. And another. Striding toward her car, she got inside and drove toward her future. A new man, even if this wasn't the one she wanted.

Arriving home, she freshened up by brushing her teeth and adding some lip gloss, mascara and perfume. The scent of the perfume overwhelmed her, so she rubbed off as much of the fragrance as she could. Seconds later, she heard a knock at her door.

Rushing to the door, she flung it open...to Max.

"What are you doing here?" she asked.

He narrowed his eyes. "What do you mean what am I doing here?"

"Well, you were at work when I left," she said.

"I left after you did," he said.

She barely resisted the urge to shift from one foot to the other. "I guess you did," she said as a young good-looking Italian man strode up from behind Max.

"Miss Sophie Taylor," he asked.

"That's me," she said. "You must be David Rinaldo."

"Yes, Signorina. Very pleased to meet you," he said, stretching to meet her gaze over Max's shoulder.

Max met her gaze. "So this is why you left early?" he asked.

"I left on time," she corrected.

"For Mr. Rinaldo."

She took a deep breath. "Yes, for a drink with David." She stepped outside her door. "Have a nice evening," she mumbled over her shoulder to Max. "Nice to meet you, David. Shall we leave?"

"Of course," David said, taking her hand. "Good night, Signore."

David led her down the stairs to the street. Sophie felt an amazing sense of relief. She was relieved to get away from Max. Relieved to escape her apartment. Exhilaration rushed through her. She was free for the moment.

David looked at her. "You look happy. Where would you like to go?"

"Anywhere," she said, feeling so happy she could hardly stand it.

David, with the seductive eyes, smiled. "I can do better than anywhere."

He took her to a quiet Italian bar and ordered wine for her and him after she told him she preferred white. A saxophonist played in the corner.

"Does this anywhere please you?" David asked.

Sophie nodded. "Yes, oh, yes. I love the music," she said, sipping her glass of pinot grigio while swaying to the beat.

"Excellent," he said. "I told Princess Bridget that I would like to meet you. I hope you don't feel I was too bold."

Surprise flashed through her. "I had no idea. I thought she assigned you to me."

He shook his head. "Assigned? I saw you the day you had tea with the princesses and asked to meet you."

"When did you possibly see me? I was with the princesses the entire time," she said.

"The door was open. I observed part of your interaction and wanted to know you better," he said.

Self-consciousness immediately rushed through her. "I can't imagine that I would have said anything to impress you during that tea."

"Your authenticity impressed me," he said.

"Hmm, my authenticity has gotten me in trouble more than once," she said.

David lifted his glass of red wine. "It won't with me."

She and David had a pleasant conversation getting to know one another better. She learned he'd achieved advanced degrees. She disclosed she'd been nearly all over the world for the sake of her job. She felt comfortable with him. Comfortable enough to agree to attend the dinner fundraiser. Not comfortable enough to allow him to kiss her good-night.

Sophie rushed into her apartment, her heart slamming against her chest. Was David her way out? Was David the man who could make her detach herself from Max? She took a deep breath. She could only hope.

Maybe a little flirtation with David was all she needed to get her on the right track. She couldn't help wondering if this was how the other half lived.

The next day, Max was in a bad mood. Sophie arrived on time to work, but she seemed distracted, even when they tossed the Nerf ball back and forth. He went out to check on the workers then returned to the office to find Sophie's desk filled with a huge arrangement of flowers. Max immediately frowned.

"Who sent those?" he asked, hoping the flowers had been sent from someone at the palace.

Sophie walked in after him. "David Rinaldo. They were a surprise."

"Pretty, aren't they?" Terri Caldwell said.

He shrugged. "A little overblown."

Terri laughed. "I don't think you can overdo when it comes to flowers," she said and gave the carnations a sniff. "Plus, they smell so beautifully. Just what did you do to inspire that man to send you these?"

Sophie's cheeks turned pink. "Nothing. All I did was drink a glass of wine with him."

"I'm just teasing you," Terri said. "He must have been impressed with you."

Max scowled. "Any man can send extravagant flowers. You better watch out if he's moving that fast."

"Why?" Sophie asked.

"Because he might want something from you that you might not want to give," he said.

"I think I'm old enough to handle what to do about that," she said.

"There's a difference between being old enough and having experience. When it comes to dealing with men on a romantic level, you're not experienced. I don't want to see you hurt."

Sophie looked at him as if he'd sprouted an extra head. "Who said anything about getting hurt? I've only been out with him once." She glanced down at the flowers. "Besides, maybe it's time for me to get some experience."

Max's gut twisted into a dozen knots. *Time for her to get some experience.* It took all of his willpower not to take those flowers Sophie had received and trash them.

He obviously felt protective and territorial about Sophie, but why? She was just his amazing assistant, right? He looked at the flowers again. No, not just trash them, burn them. Anger burned up inside of him, which meant he was more emotionally involved than he should be. He needed to do something about his feelings. But it wasn't as if he could order her not to go out with this guy. For Pete's sake, where had these thoughts come from? He needed to get himself under control.

Sophie gave the flowers another sniff then sank down into her desk chair. Max had never seen Sophie exhibit the slightest interest in another man and now she was acting all girly about David Rinaldo. Max had always counted on Sophie being sensible, emotionally detached to other men and focused on being his assistant.

He'd counted on her staying focused on being the best assistant he'd ever had. The notion had brought him comfort. Now he wasn't feeling so sure. The trailer felt as if it were closing in on him. He needed to go outside. "I've got to double-check the grade on the road. I'll be back later," he said and left, letting the door slam behind him.

Sophie stared at her laptop screen, scanning her eyes over the line she'd pretended to read for the fifth time. She heard Terri snicker and bit her lip to keep from responding.

"Looks like Max is allergic to flowers," Terri said, wandering to Sophie's desk. "Especially if some other man is giving them to you."

"Don't start," Sophie said. "He's just probably feeling extra protective because of the scooter accident."

"That sounded more like jealousy than just overprotectiveness to me. You might finally be getting the man's attention. Good for you."

"I'm not going out with David to get Max's attention.

He's a nice, interesting guy. I had fun with him. It was a nice change," she retorted.

"Well, I'm glad you're having fun. You are way over-due." Terri gave a snicker. "And it's so much fun watching Max squirm."

Sophie *was* surprised by Max's reaction, but she couldn't believe that he was truly jealous. Max had been given every opportunity in the world to make a move on her, and the one time he had, he'd apologized and said it was a mistake. No. Terri was wrong on this one.

Sophie was going to try to enjoy David's attention. It was a refreshing change.

One day later, Sophie received a call from Bridget. "Meet me for lunch and shopping tomorrow. We can discuss delicious David and your upcoming appearance at the historical awareness dinner."

Sophie felt an itchy discomfort. "Appearance?" Sophie echoed. "I'm not supposed to give a speech, am I?"

"Oh, no, of course not. You'll just be introduced as one of the honored guests and sit at the head table. But it's a great opportunity for a new dress and shoes."

Sophie had been planning on wearing the little black dress she wore for any and every occasion that sounded formal-ish. "I'd love to meet you for lunch sometime, but I'm swamped with work right now. Since I had the accident, I've been doing a lot of catch-up."

"Well, surely Max could spare you for one afternoon. We need to move on this, in case you need alterations," she said in a firm voice. "And of course, the day of the event, the palace stylist will do your hair and makeup."

"Whoa," Sophie said. "I don't really wear that much makeup."

"Of course you don't, but the cameras can wash you out," Bridget said. "Shall I have Stefan speak to Max on your behalf?"

"Oh, no, absolutely not," Sophie said, cringing at the thought. "Why would I need to be concerned about cameras?"

Bridget giggled. "Because you're a guest of honor, silly. Plus, everyone will know you're involved in the road improvement project and trust me, the whole country is thrilled about that."

"If this crowd is going to be interested in the road recovery project, then why didn't you ask Max?" Sophie asked.

"Oh, I've asked him to make a half dozen appearances and he refuses every time. You're much more sociable. Now, you're sure I shouldn't ask Stefan—"

"No, no. I just—" She broke off, frustrated, waving at Terri as the woman entered the work trailer. "I'm just more of a low-key, low-maintenance kind of person. I don't really think I'll need to shop for a new dress for the dinner."

"Shopping?" Terri said. "You should definitely get a new dress. When is the last time you got one?"

"Excuse me," she said to Bridget and covered the phone. "This is Princess Bridget inviting me to shop tomorrow. There's no way Max will go for it. We're so busy—"

"I'll cover for you," Terri said.

Sophie blinked. "What?"

"I'll cover for you. I was supposed to take tomorrow off to do some touring with the hubby, but since he's decided to stay until next week, I can put it off another day. Go shopping."

"But—"

"Go!" Terri said.

Sophie sighed and uncovered the phone. "Your highness, it looks like I can join you tomorrow after all."

"Splendid," Bridget said. "We'll have a wonderful time."

Sophie hung up the phone and met Terri's gaze. "I'm not sure what I've gotten myself into."

Chapter Six

The next day, Sophie left the office as soon as Terri arrived.

"Enjoy it. You don't get out enough. Splurge a little," Terri said.

"We'll see," Sophie said as she headed for her tiny rental car. She wasn't that worried about the expense because she rarely had time for shopping, and she had a nice chunk of savings and investments. The advantage to working all the time was that she had little opportunity to spend the money she made.

Sophie drove to her apartment to change into a pair of black slacks and a white blouse before meeting Princess Bridget. Just as she decided to walk to the café, her cell phone rang.

"Hello?"

"Miss Taylor, this is Sean Stapleton. I'll pick you up for your appointment with Her Highness in ten minutes," a man said.

"That's really not necessary. I can walk it in the same amount of time," she said.

He cleared his throat. "Princess Bridget forbids you to walk to the restaurant," he said.

"Forbids?" she said.

"I found the wording a bit strong myself, but she doesn't want another accident—"

Sophie rolled her eyes. Ever since her encounter with the scooter, everyone seemed to be paranoid about her crossing the street. "Okay, thank you. I'll be downstairs. During the moments she waited for the driver, Sophie experienced second and third thoughts about accepting the princess's invitation to attend the historical awareness dinner.

Dressing up and going out hadn't been part of her practice. If there was any time left at the end of the day, she usually either read a book or caught up on a favorite television show. Her social life was nearly nonexistent. If the company hosted a holiday or end-of-project party, the attire was jeans and the beverage served was ice cold beer.

She suspected her bruised ego from being rejected by Max had influenced her decision. Although she'd enjoyed David enough, the whole thing was starting to make her feel a little edgy.

Seconds later, the driver appeared and assisted her into the car. As she'd pointed out to him, the ride was so short she barely spent any time in the car. At the café, she was led to a corner table with a view of the colorful street. A few moments later, Princess Bridget arrived, wearing a bright pink dress with a matching hat and heels. She nodded and smiled at several of the café's customers on her way to the table.

Sophie stood to greet her and considered attempting a curtsey.

As if Bridget could read her mind, she shook her head. "Absolutely no curtsey." She gave Sophie a warm embrace then sat down. "This is going to be such a treat for me. I've been stuck on the ranch, and I use the term loosely. We have cattle, chickens and horses, but I told my dear husband that I'm drawing the line at goats and sheep. Besides, he expects me to learn to feed and tend the animals. I think feeding and tending the twins is quite enough," she chuckled. "Has he lost his mind? But at least I can tell he's very happy. The only thing that would make him happier is if Chantaine had a baseball or football team. That's for another day. In the meantime, you and I can have a lovely lunch and shop. What looks good to you?" she asked as she glanced at the menu.

After a delicious meal of sea scallops and a glass of wine, Sophie was full to the brim. "This was wonderful. I'm usually eating a sandwich I packed for lunch. Thank you for inviting me."

"My pleasure. Of course, the best is yet to come."

"Oh, I don't think I have room for dessert," Sophie said, patting her stomach.

"Not dessert, silly. The shopping," Bridget said.

Sophie felt a rush of nerves. "I think you may be more of a risk-taker when it comes to fashion. I tend to go the conservative, classic route."

"Well, here's your opportunity to break out of your shell," Bridget said.

Sophie liked her shell. It felt safe in there. "Seriously, I went shopping at Christmas, but didn't buy anything for myself."

"That's fine. That's why you're going with me. I'll make sure you don't buy anything too boring or practical." When Sophie opened her mouth to protest, Bridget lifted her hand and shook her head. "Answer one question. What was the last article of clothing you purchased?"

Sophie racked her brain then winced as she remembered. "Besides the blue dress I bought for tea, a pair of pants with zippers that would allow you to turn them into shorts."

Bridget blinked and shook her head. "I rest my case."

After that, Sophie felt as if she'd been caught in a whirlwind. Somehow in the search for a dress, she purchased a pair of skinny jeans, two stylish tops and a pair of sandals with heels. Sophie kept gravitating toward the black dresses, while Bridget led her to bright colors. She wasn't sure how it happened, but she found herself staring in the mirror at the image of a woman wearing a knockout red dress and nude heels.

"Now tell me, is that perfect, or what?" Bridget asked, clearly proud of herself.

"I don't know what to say. I never would have chosen this." Sophie still couldn't believe she was looking at her own reflection.

"Fabulous. Now let's see if we can find one more dress—"

"Oh, no. I think I'm done. Really."

Bridget pouted. "But what will you wear for your next big event? You can't wear the same outfit twice in a row."

"Let's just deal with one event at a time," Sophie said. "And thank you. I already told you I'm not much of a shopper, but you sure know how to make it fun."

Bridget's lips lifted in a soft smile. "One of my little skills. Are you sure I can't talk you into one more dress? There are two more shops I'd love to show you."

"Not today, but thank you very much. You've been much too generous with your time and expertise," Sophie said and wondered if the Devereaux sisters knew how lucky they were to have each other. The thought stabbed at a tender place inside her. She had never allowed herself to wish for a brother or sister of her own. Her mother had always clearly felt pressured by being a single parent that she wouldn't have been able to take on the care of another child.

The sad feeling haunted her, but she refused to let it drag her down after she'd had such a wonderful experience with Bridget. The princess's chauffeur drove Sophie to her apartment and Bridget gave her a quick hug.

"Have a nice, peaceful evening," Bridget joked. "Think of me chasing the twins and the chickens. Ciao."

"Ciao, your highness," Sophie said and walked to her apartment.

As soon as Sophie stepped inside her apartment, she pulled her red dress from her bag and swished and swirled in front of the full-length mirror. She laughed to herself. "Oh, wow," she whispered.

"Oh, wow," Max said from behind her.

Panic swept through her. "Uh," was all she could manage. "How'd you get in here?"

"You gave me your key," he said.

"Oh, yeah," she said and tried to regain her equilibrium. "What's up?"

He studied her for a long moment. "I've been thinking."

Her stomach clenched. "About what?"

"About what kind of charity we should do here in Chantaine. I think we should make a regional center for kids with orthopedic and birth injuries and improve handicap accessibility."

She bit her lip. "I like it. Where'd you get the idea?"

"Saw a kid who couldn't go anywhere today. This place is not handicap accessible."

"That's a pretty tall order," she said. "How can we do it?"

"It will take more work than usual. Terri said she and her husband would help. He's pretty handy." He searched her gaze. "You may be too busy with your new social commitments, though…"

She frowned at him. "Just because I'm making a social commitment or two doesn't mean I won't be able to step up for what you're asking."

"Good to know." He nodded.

"Princess Bridget said she asked you to make a few appearances and you turned her down flat."

He shook his head. "They sounded pretty useless to me."

"Your appearance may have raised some money for a valuable cause."

"Sounds kind of superficial to me."

"Maybe," she said. "Or not."

He met her gaze. "What makes you so sure?"

"You should use your royal powers for good."

He scowled sat her. "What royal powers?"

"You technically have royal blood. Not everyone does. That means you have special powers. Royal powers," she said in a low voice.

"Sounds like bull to me. I've never believed in the power of being royal and I still don't now."

"But other people believe in the royal thing. The idea of a prince and princess makes them feel better. It gives them hope."

He frowned again.

"You need to give people a break. We all need to be inspired, and you are a very inspiring man."

He lifted a doubtful eyebrow. "You think so?"

"Yes, I do," she said confidently. "I also think the best way to earn some money for handicapped kids is by holding an event that you attend. And your best bet is Bridget. If anyone can pull a charity event together quickly, she can."

He rolled his eyes. "So, you're saying I have to make nice to Princess Bridget?"

"No. I'm just saying you have to ask her for help."

"That's the same as making nice."

Sophie shrugged. "That's a matter of opinion. Bridget has skills just as you have skills. She can throw a great party. Neither you nor I can do that."

"This royal thing is a whole different world," he said.

"Well, you're always conquering new worlds," she rebutted.

"Hmm. Maybe. I'll think about it."

"Well, you have other options. You could always hold a bake sale or a car wash. Those may not make a lot of money, but—"

"Okay, okay," he grumbled. "I'll talk to Bridget."

He glanced at the red dress she'd hung on the back of the door. "Nice dress. David Rinaldo is a lucky guy. See you tomorrow," Max said as he walked out the door.

"Nice dress…David's a lucky guy," she echoed and scowled at the door. "*You* could have been the lucky guy."

Max didn't sleep well that night. He kept thinking about Sophie and that sexy dress, and the fact that she would be wearing it for David Rinaldo. Once David got a good look at Sophie in that dress, Max was pretty sure the man would try to get her into his bed. Any man in his right mind would do the same.

The notion gave him indigestion. Rising from his bed, he went to the bathroom and chomped down some antacids. Chasing them with water, he temporarily gave up on sleeping and pulled out his laptop. He played with a few design ideas for a meeting place for disabled kids.

He'd like to secure a bottom floor of a building. It would also be great if they could put together a small outdoor playground. Max had a friend who specialized in these kinds of renovations. He would give him a call.

Lost in exploring his ideas, he barely noticed the passing of time until the first light of dawn slid through his window. *Morning already? Great,* he thought. He was going to feel like yesterday's coffee by the afternoon. Sighing, he ran his hand through his hair and rose from the couch. At least he had some ideas for the charity project and he'd gotten Sophie off his mind for a while.

Max took a shower and grabbed a cup of coffee before he left for work. He was early, but there was always something to do. In this case, *something* happened an hour after he arrived. He spent the better part of the morning fixing a broken piece of machinery. By lunchtime, he was dirty, cranky and hungry.

He entered the work trailer to see David Rinaldo propped against Sophie's desk and her face lit up like it was Christmas. His mood went from bad to worse.

"Hey," he interrupted.

"Oh, hi," Sophie said and rose from her desk. "I'm not sure you were properly introduced. David Rinaldo," she said, lifting her hand toward the man who clearly hadn't spent his morning sweating over a piece of machinery, "this is my boss, Max Caldwell." She nodded toward Max. "Good news. I've caught up on all the paperwork and work orders and plans for the next week. Were you able to fix the sandblaster?"

"I didn't have the right part, but I made a workaround. Do we have a lunch delivery on the way?"

"I was just going to place an order when David arrived. He wants to take me for a little picnic, if that's okay with you," she said.

"I know a beautiful scenic spot not far from here," David said. "But I promise I won't keep her too long."

Max bet David knew of quite a few scenic spots on the island.

"Oh, but that leaves you without lunch," Sophie said to Max then turned to David. "Do you think you might have an extra sandwich in that basket?"

Max shook his head. He didn't want anything from David. "Not necessary. I'll find something."

Sophie bit her lip. "But—"

"There's plenty in the basket. The palace packed it, so I'm sure we couldn't eat it all. I'll bring it in," David said and left.

"Hey, you don't need to—" Max broke off and rubbed his face with his hand. "Nice surprise," he said in a dry tone. "Your boyfriend showing up with a picnic basket."

"It is nice, and you're right. A complete surprise. I don't know what to say. I don't think I've even ever been on a picnic with a man. And he's not my boyfriend. He's my friend," she told him then smiled. "But it's fun, isn't it?"

"I guess," he said then washed his hands at the small sink in the corner of the trailer. "Fair warning. A man doesn't take you for a picnic just because he wants to be your friend."

"How would you know?" she countered. "How many times have you taken a woman on a picnic?"

"Never," he admitted, and it made him feel like a smuck. He'd never had to work too hard at wooing the ladies. That romantic stuff seemed like crap to him. Good conversation and a good time in bed were more important, and making sure he kept things honest with the ladies.

Toting the basket, David came in the door with Terri walking behind him. "What's this?" Terri asked.

"David is sharing some of our picnic with Max," Sophie said and introduced David to Terri.

David opened the basket. "Would you care for wine? There are two bottles," David said.

"No. That's okay. I'm okay with a sandwich," Max said, feeling more irritable with each passing moment.

"Here's a croissant. Chicken, a pasta salad, cheese, a chocolate pastry and cherries. Will that do?" David asked.

"Sure," Max said with a short nod. It was all he could do not to grind his teeth. *Cherries.* He couldn't avoid the sexual comparison, but he tried. "Thanks. You two go ahead on your picnic."

Both of them left, thank goodness. Max immediately took his food to his desk and took a bite of chicken.

"Isn't that the sweetest thing?" Terri asked. "I'm so glad she's getting out and that someone's paying attention to her. She sure deserves it."

Max swallowed hard over the chicken in his throat. "Hmm."

"She does," Terri said. "The poor girl has worked like a dog with no social life. I'm glad there's a man giving her a little special attention. Aren't you?"

Max chewed on another bite of chicken. "I guess," he said.

"I guess?" Terri echoed in disapproval. "She's a young woman. She works hard. She's a darling woman. Isn't it good that some man appreciates her?"

Max frowned, feeling torn in a dozen directions. "Maybe," he said. "Sophie's a good woman."

"That's an understatement," Terri said. "Sophie is a rock star. And more than one man is going to realize that and try to win her heart."

He felt as if Terri were issuing a warning that he didn't want to receive. "I can't disagree with you," he said.

Max chomped down the rest of the lunch, nearly choking on the cherries, but he made himself chew the sweet fruit and swallow it. With every bite, he thought of Sophie. He couldn't help thinking about how much he wanted her. It was crazy and he needed to get it out of his system.

Despite finishing his lunch, he still felt empty. He still wanted Sophie. It had nothing to do with food and he had no idea how to rid himself of the gosh-awful longing.

When Sophie returned to the office trailer, she was giggling with delight.

"How was the wine?" he asked.

"I only drank a little," she said. "Because I have to work this afternoon. But whew, it sure tasted good."

He nodded, wishing he had been the guy to make her want wine more than beer. "Good dessert, too."

"Delicious," she said. "Extremely delicious. I never knew dating could be this much fun," she said and spun around before she took her seat.

Max felt a terrible sense of regret. He wished he had been the one to make her love being courted. Why hadn't he? He felt like a dud.

On Saturday, Sophie was driven to the palace for a mani-pedi. She was surprised when Eve, Pippa and Bridget showed up for the pedicure.

"How are you all feeling?" Sophie asked as each of the women dipped their feet into swirling hot water.

"I needed this," Eve said.

"So did I," Pippa chirped.

"I've always said a pedicure is underrated," Bridget added and sighed.

Sophie took her turn soaking her feet in the tub and leaned her head against the backrest. She noticed a control for the massage chair and pushed the button.

Seconds later, she heard the low hum of massage from the other chairs. "So, how are the babies?" Bridget asked.

"My nanny has Amelie at the moment," Pippa said. "If she needs milk, I've pumped some for her. That said, I have nothing against formula. I'm confident my baby will thrive either way."

"Hear, hear," Eve said. "Although my feeding is going well, I wouldn't mind a break now and then."

"And then there are shoes," Bridget said. "Because not all of us are obsessed with breast milk."

"I've never been fond of overly high heels. I like a good pair of riding boots, though," Eve said, her eyes closed as she rested her head against the back of her chair.

"My perfect shoe," Pippa said, "would be both elegant and comfortable. I would love for someone to design such a shoe. Bridget, there's no way I would wear the high-heeled shoes you do."

"I'm used to it," Bridget said, sloshing her feet in the swirling water. "I've walked in high heels through sand. It's training. Do you know how easy it is to walk on marble after you've trudged through wet sand?"

"I never thought of it that way," Pippa said. "And I never will again. It's clearly not important enough for me."

Sophie couldn't quite swallow a snicker.

"Is that a laugh?" Bridget asked with a disapproving tone.

"Sorry. Couldn't help it. Not everyone can wear heels like you do."

"Agreed," Eve said.

"I second that," Pippa said. "Perhaps you should be given a special award. The Princess who can wear heels in any situation."

"You're ridiculous," Bridget snapped back. "And you shouldn't mock me."

"We're not," Eve said. "We're admiring you."

"Why don't I feel admired?" Bridget asked.

"Because we have to mock you to make up for our inability," Sophie said without thinking. A second later, she wondered if she had offended Bridget. "Maybe I should have phrased that differently."

"No." Bridget snickered. "I think you phrased it perfectly. But enough of that. How are our babies sleeping?"

"Not bad," Eve said. "June Bug seems to crave his nighttime sleep, which makes me happy."

"Amelie is pretty good, too. She's nowhere near sleeping through the night, but she's excellent about going back to sleep."

"Does Stefan mind you calling the heir June Bug?" Bridget asked.

"No. We call him all kinds of silly things like lovey, sweetie pie. June Bug is just one of many. Don't share it with the press," she joked. "When he gets older you'll have to call him something else," Bridget said.

"Yes," Eve said. "But that's later. Now we can treat him like a baby, thank goodness."

"Well, speaking of heirs, I received a shocking call from our half brother," Bridget said.

Curious, but determined to be discreet, Sophie kept her mouth shut.

"Really?" Pippa said. "No insult to you, Sophie, but he hasn't been very friendly. I mean, we truly appreciate what he's doing with roads on the north island, but I've gotten the feeling he doesn't approve of us."

"I think he doesn't quite know what to do in this situation," Sophie piped in. "He's never had any brothers or sisters."

"I can see how we would throw him for a loop. The Devereauxes can be a little loony at times," Eve said in her Texas drawl.

"We're not loony," Bridget insisted, appearing indignant. "We're just—" She broke off as if she couldn't come up with the perfect word.

"Unique," Pippa offered. "Yet, at the same time we're like everyone else." She chuckled. "Because everyone is a little crazy, yes?"

Sophie couldn't help laughing along with Pippa.

"Hmm. I'm not sure I like being called crazy," Bridget said, but she was smiling. "But anyways, Maxwell Carter called me to ask if I would help put together a charity event to support his plan to remodel a center for handicapped children downtown. I must say I am bowled over. Although we all appreciate what he's doing for our roads, I never would have expected this additional generosity from him."

Sophie felt her heart stir. "He puts up a good front that he doesn't care, but he does care more than you might think."

"I'm quite impressed," Bridget said.

"So am I," Eve said. "I love this plan. My time is limited right now, but let me know if there's something I can do."

Pippa nodded. "You've got the same offer from me."

"Perfect," Bridget said and glanced at Sophie. "Maybe this will be another event for you and David to attend."

"David Rinaldo?" Eve asked and gave a nod of approval. "He's a good guy. Stefan really respects him."

"Romance is in the air," Bridget said with a smile.

"Friendship is in the air," Sophie corrected.

An hour later, Sophie was led to the palace stylist. She'd enjoyed the mani-pedi, but the makeup made her a little crazy. "Are you sure this isn't a bit much?" she asked Bridget as the palace stylist applied her cosmetics.

"You're looking beautiful. Once you see the photos, you'll be glad you did this," Bridget said.

"Seems like a lot of plaster to me," Sophie said.

Bridget laughed. "She has no idea about plaster." She nudged the stylist.

"You have beautiful skin," the stylist said. "I just want to make it look better for the photographers. Compared to others, you take so little time."

"You're very kind," Sophie said.

"Actually, I'm not," he said. "I've applied makeup for many others who needed far more than you."

"Then, thank you very much," she said.

"You're welcome," he said with a wink. "But you were easy. Once you put on your red dress, every man in the room will jump at the opportunity to meet you."

Every man in the room. The prospect made her nervous. She wasn't at all accustomed to receiving that much attention. At the same time, she couldn't help thinking that the man whose attention she most wanted wouldn't even be in the room.

Chapter Seven

"Would you like another drink?" David asked as he skimmed his hand over Sophie's bare shoulder and leaned closer to her.

His proximity made her uneasy. Until tonight, she'd enjoyed the friendly flirtation, but it seemed he was touching her much more frequently and sitting a little too close, allowing his thigh to slide against hers. Sophie found herself trying to edge away as subtly as she could.

Relieved when the dinner was concluded and David drove her to her apartment, she nearly leapt from the car. "Well, this has been a lovely evening. Thank you so much for escorting me," she said as they climbed the stairs to her apartment.

"It doesn't have to end," he said in a low, seductive voice. "If you invite me in."

Yikes, she thought and covered a big yawn. "Oh, this has been a very long day. I'm afraid I'm totally worn out." She put her key in her door and glanced over her shoulder. "Thank you again—"

He leaned in and caught her lips with his before she could stop him. Automatically pulling back, she cleared her throat. "Thank you again."

"I'll call you soon," he promised.

Sophie closed the door behind her and leaned against it. *Well, darn.* This flirtation distraction wasn't working out nearly like she'd planned. How was she supposed to have a successful flirtation if she didn't even want the man to kiss her? Sighing, she unzipped the dress and hung it up. It seemed to mock her very hopes and dreams from the hanger.

It was obvious she was going to have to tell David that she wasn't interested in anything but friendship with him. Frustrated, she got into the shower and washed away her perfect makeup and hairstyle. Time to go back to being herself. She just wished she wanted to kiss David. But instead, Max still hung in her mind…and that kiss.

Sunday morning, Max rose and drank his coffee in the kitchen. He still had to work on the designs for the center for handicapped children. He could have stayed in his apartment and tooled around, but he decided he'd rather go to the office so he could print off some of the options.

As he drove toward the work trailer, he noticed the

road was progressing well, but not as well as he'd hoped. They would be hard-pressed to finish on schedule. Max halfway noticed the beauty of the foliage and the glimpses of the rocky coast and azure ocean, but he was more interested in making headway on the plans for the new center.

Pulling into the parking lot, he noticed Sophie's car parked next to the trailer. That's right, he thought. The big date with Stefan's advisor had taken place last night. The knowledge had driven him so nuts that he'd spent most of the evening at the gym, wearing himself out with a workout. He'd tried not to think about that guy seducing Sophie, but he hadn't been successful. Truth was he hadn't slept well in days, but he was doing his best to ignore the fact.

Curious as to why she had decided to come to the office, he entered the trailer and saw her focused on computer work. "Hey, what are you doing here?"

"Making sure I stay ahead of the curve," she said, not looking up at him. "I don't want to get behind. Why are you here?"

"Working on the plans for the center for handicapped children. I want to print off some drafts. Easier for me to compare," he said.

She nodded, but still didn't meet his gaze. "Good idea."

He watched her for a moment. Her body was tense and erect and she didn't wear a speck of makeup. Violet shadows formed circles underneath her eyes. Max went to the coffeemaker, which held half a pot, and poured himself a cup. "So how was the dinner last night?"

"Crab and steak. Excellent food for that kind of event," she said, still not looking at him.

"And what about David? How'd that go?" he asked, taking a sip of the strong brew.

She finally met his gaze. "Do we have to discuss this?"

Whoa, he thought. "No. I was just curious. He was Mr. Picnic last week."

"That was last week," she said with a frown and returned her gaze to her computer screen.

Max took another sip and studied her a moment longer. "He didn't hurt you or try to force you into anything, did he?"

Sophie sighed and looked at him. "No. I just want to be friends with him and I think he may want—" She bit her lip. "More."

Max nodded, relief flooding his body. He didn't overthink his reaction. "Poor guy," he said, even though he didn't feel one bit of sympathy for David.

She winced. "I guess," she said.

Max went with his instincts. He would question them later. "Well, how about if we work for awhile then hit the beach this afternoon?"

She blinked at him. "The beach?"

"Yeah," he said. "How often have you gone since we've been here?"

"Not once," she said.

He shrugged. "So you wanna go?"

She stared at him for a long moment. "Okay," she said. "Why not?"

Max worked through the next couple of hours, printed off his design options and shut down his laptop. He turned to Sophie. "Ready to go to the beach?"

She looked up at him. "Yes, but my bathing suit is at my apartment."

"Let's go," he said. "We're burning daylight."

Max led the way in his rental car until Sophie took a different turn to get to her apartment. Drumming his fingers on the steering wheel, he thought about what he should take for their trip to the beach. Beer. Did he have wine? Could he get it quickly if he didn't have it?

Why was he second-guessing himself?

He gave a quick call to Sophie. "You bring the towels. I'll bring the beverages, and I'll drive."

"I can put together a couple sandwiches," she said.

"Offer accepted," he said. At the same time, he thought his plan was nowhere near a gourmet picnic created by the palace.

Max was nothing if he wasn't quick, so he grabbed his trunks and whipped into a wine store. He grabbed two bottles along with beer, ice and a wine opener. Moments later, he pulled in front of Sophie's apartment. He tried to remember the last time he'd taken a woman to the beach. He usually just took a woman to dinner and to bed. Max wondered why he felt such a kick of anticipation.

Moments later, Sophie burst from the front of her apartment building carrying a couple of bags and wearing a big smile. The smile got to Max. He reached over and opened the car door. "Come on in."

OFFICIAL OPINION POLL

Dear Reader,

Since you are a book enthusiast, we would like to know what you think.

Inside you will find a short Opinion Poll. Please participate in our poll by sharing your opinion on 3 subjects that are very important to all of us.

To thank you for your participation, we would like to send you **2 FREE BOOKS** and **2 FREE GIFTS!**

Please enjoy them with our compliments.

Sincerely,

Pam Powers

For Your Reading Pleasure...

Get 2 FREE BOOKS where contemporary heroines find the balance between their work life and personal life on the way to true love.

Free

YOUR OPINION POLL
THANK-YOU FREE GIFTS INCLUDE:

▶ **2 HARLEQUIN® SPECIAL EDITION BOOKS**

▶ **2 LOVELY SURPRISE GIFTS**

OFFICIAL OPINION POLL

YOUR OPINION COUNTS!
Please check TRUE or FALSE below to express your opinion about the following statements:

Q1 Do you believe in "true love"?

"TRUE LOVE HAPPENS ONLY ONCE IN A LIFETIME."
○ TRUE
○ FALSE

Q2 Do you think marriage has any value in today's world?

"YOU CAN BE TOTALLY COMMITTED TO SOMEONE WITHOUT BEING MARRIED."
○ TRUE
○ FALSE

Q3 What kind of books do you enjoy?

"A GREAT NOVEL MUST HAVE A HAPPY ENDING."
○ TRUE
○ FALSE

YES! I have placed my sticker in the space provided below. Please send me the **2 FREE books** and **2 FREE gifts** for which I qualify. I understand that I am under no obligation to purchase anything further, as explained on the back of this card.

235/335 HDL FVN6

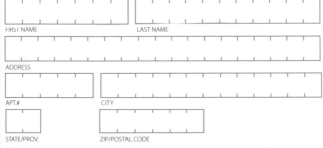

FIRST NAME

LAST NAME

ADDRESS

APT.#

CITY

STATE/PROV.

ZIP/POSTAL CODE

HSE-I1-03/13
Printed in the U.S.A.
© 2012 HARLEQUIN ENTERPRISES LIMITED.

She slid inside the passenger seat and crammed the bags in the floorboard. "Ready," she said.

"Then we're off." He drove toward the shore. "I hear there are several beaches. One is for families. One allows nudity." He paused a half beat. "One is a little further north and not so busy."

"Let's go north," she said.

He shifted the manual shift into second. "Your wish is my command."

"Yeah," she said in disbelief and lowered her window. The wind whipped through the vehicle and Max lowered his passenger window, too. The breeze was refreshing. It made him wonder why he'd waited so long to go to the beach. After all, the ocean was so close.

"This is wonderful," Sophie said. "The ocean smells so good."

"Can't disagree," Max said.

"Life is short. I'm thinking we all should enjoy what life offers. Next year, I may not be near the ocean."

He suddenly realized what she was saying. They'd worked so many projects together, in so many interesting places, but they'd worked so hard that they'd rarely explored and enjoyed the countries they'd visited.

"True," he said. "The beach is calling."

He drove north and pulled into a public beach access. "This okay?"

She nodded.

He pulled the drinks and ice from the car and grabbed one of her bags. They hiked up to the beach. The hot sand sank under their feet. They trudged toward the shore where the sand was more tightly packed.

Sophie pulled out the towels, tossed one at him, set hers on the sand and pulled off her cover-up. She wore a sensible black one-piece, but Max couldn't deny a burning curiosity about her tight, slim little body. Plopping down on her blanket, she stared at the ocean for a long moment.

"Nice view," Max said, but he was looking at the woman beside him.

She smiled at him, clearly missing his point. "That, it is."

Max half-chuckled to himself. "Wanna go in?"

A sliver of reticence crossed her face. "I think I want to just look at it for awhile first."

"Afraid?" he asked as he pulled a beer from the bag. "Want one?"

"Not yet," she said. "And not really afraid. I'm just not the best swimmer."

"You can't swim?" he asked, surprised. Sophie was so competent he hadn't considered she'd have a weakness in any area, especially something practical like swimming.

"I can swim," she corrected him. "But with the exception of that trip to the Great Barrier Reef last year when I wore a life jacket and was supervised by the tour agents, I haven't done a lot of ocean swimming." She sighed and wove her fingers through the sugar-white sand. "The truth is I went swimming on a day trip with a friend and got caught in an undertow. I swallowed a lot of water."

"Well, I can't let you keep thinking about that," he said, putting down his beer, grabbing her hand and lifting her to her feet.

"What are you talking about?" she asked, tugging away from him.

"It may sound like amateur psychology, but the best way to deal with a bad memory is to replace it with a good experience. Let's go."

"Oh, I don't know," she said, but moved along beside him as he led the way to the water. "Besides, what if it's cold?"

"You'll warm up after a few minutes," he said, scooping her into his arms and walking into the surf, which was cooler than he'd expected. She gave a half-muted squeal that made him laugh. "The thing you have to remember about the ocean is that it's not the same all the time. It can be stormy. There can be dangerous riptides. Or it can be calm like today. Look around," he said and pointed up the beach. "See those people over there? The water is nearly up to their waists and they're floating on their backs." He lowered her into the cool water.

Her eyes grew round and she sucked in a quick breath. "Yikes, this is cold. You could have warned me." She crossed her hands over her chest and hugged her arms. She stepped into a hole under the water, putting her off balance.

Max caught her before she tumbled into the water. "See, it's not that bad."

She glared at him. "You could have given me a little time to get used to the idea."

He laughed. "Can't do that. We're burning daylight. I don't know when we'll get another chance to get out here again."

"Well, I guess that's true," she conceded and looked around. "This really is an interesting island. The people, the variety of the landscape. Rocks on one beach and trees on another. Are you glad you came to meet your half siblings?"

He shrugged, feeling conflicted. "I guess so. It's a complicated relationship."

"I understand Bridget is gearing up to help you with a fundraiser," she said.

He glanced at her in surprise. "I just talked to her a few days ago."

"She's a mover and shaker when it comes to social events, and it's not as if she has months to pull this off. If you think about it, the more she talks about it, the better for the charity project."

"Okay. Unless it's a beer and burger party, she's probably better at this stuff than I am," he said. "And now one more thing to take care of your previous bad experience in the water," he said as he leaned closer to her.

"What's that?" she asked, and he saw her gaze dip to his mouth.

Max was tempted to go ahead and kiss her, but he had a feeling he'd better take his time with sweet Sophie. "Hold your breath," he said.

Her eyes widened in shock. "Oh, you're not going to dunk me."

He shook his head. "No. You are."

"I'm what?" she asked.

"You're going to dunk your own head under the water," he said, then added before she could protest, "I dare you."

She glowered at him. "You would."

"Hey, you nagged me into coming to Chantaine," he said. "Fair is fair."

"Okay, okay," she said and sank under the water, then burst to the surface.

She took his breath away. Her hair slicked back and her skin glistening with water, she reminded him of a mermaid. He wondered how he could have missed the beauty of her skin and the glow of her cheeks, how dark her eyelashes were. He felt like an idiot.

"Done," she said with a laugh. "Now I want to sit on my towel." She slipped away before he could grab her hand and she ran from the water. Something inside him felt a little lighter at the sight of her skipping through the water.

Sophie didn't know what was going on, but she liked it. Mostly. She'd never seen Max look at her quite that way before. At one point, she'd thought he was going to kiss her. A strange combination of adrenaline and sweetness rushed through her. She'd been waiting so long. Was Max *really* finally seeing her? Or would this turn into another fake-out?

Perhaps she was imagining it. Her stomach sank. Struggling with her emotions, she mashed down all the risk and scariness of the situation. Terri would tell her to enjoy it. *Don't worry. Enjoy,* Terri would say. Sophie tried to take her friend's imaginary advice.

Sophie watched Max as he walked toward her, his wide football-player shoulders moving from one side to the other. Far too attractive for his own good, he sank down beside her with a cocky grin. "I got you into the water. Betcha like the ocean better now, don't you?"

It was hard to resist him. "Maybe," she said.

"Maybe?" he challenged, nudging her with his elbow.

"Okay, you've given me another memory. It may take a few more to completely obliterate that one where I got caught in the undertow." She looked away, sifting her fingers through the sand then she looked back at him. "But this was a good start."

"Ready for a beer? Or do you want wine?" he asked.

"I'll take a beer," she said and leaned back on her elbows. "Do you remember the first time you saw the ocean?"

"Yep," he said. "We went to the Eastern Shore when I was ten. Loved it right off the bat. Drowned out my parents' arguments."

She took a sip of the brew and looked at him. "That must have been hard on you."

"Yeah," Max said then gave a faint smile. "But the waves were great."

"The first time I saw the ocean was the time I got pulled into the undertow," she said. "It helped to visit the Great Barrier Reef. That kinda forced me to give it another try. It helped having the life jacket and all that supervision. And seeing the fish. That was just amazing."

"You never told me you were afraid of the ocean," Max said.

"I'm not technically afraid. Remember I snorkeled the Great Barrier Reef," she said.

He nodded. "True. That's pretty impressive."

"I would have felt like a real wuss if I hadn't," she admitted.

He met her gaze. "I've never thought of you as a wuss."

"We all have our secret fears," she said and took another sip of beer. "So, for each drink of beer, we have to answer a question."

"Why ruin a good beer?" he asked.

"C'mon," she said. "It'll be fun. Your favorite color?" she asked. "Wait. I can answer that. Blue."

"How'd you know?"

She shrugged. "Just noticed. You always pick it when given a choice."

"What about you? What's your favorite color?" he asked.

"Guess," she said.

He glanced at her bathing suit. "Black?"

She tossed him a dark look.

"Oops. Pink?"

"I have two. Blue and green. I like green because it makes me feel calm."

"Okay," he said. "Favorite flower?"

"I really love a combination bouquet. Roses, carnations, greenery. I like something that smells good and lasts." She smiled and pumped her feet. "What about you?"

"Flowers?" he asked. He'd never even thought about it. "Something that won't make me sneeze. Something in the ground. Maybe a bush. My adoptive mother had one. Hydran—something."

"Hydrangea. They're beautiful. Excellent choice. They can be pink, white, blue, purple."

"She had blue ones. Big flowers with lots of blooms. She watered them every day."

"Does she still have them?" Sophie asked.

"Yeah, still does." He sighed and took another drink. "Favorite food?"

"Chocolate mousse cake," she said quickly.

"That was fast," he said.

"That was an easy choice. What's your favorite?"

"It's a toss-up between ribs and steak."

"No sweets for you," she teased.

"Maybe I can persuade you to share," he said, leaning toward her, making her catch her breath.

"I don't know about that. I love chocolate mousse cake," she said and took a sip of her beer. "Favorite movie?"

"Crank."

"I've never seen it, but I suspect mayhem and murder."

"What about you?"

She hesitated, because she knew he would tease her relentlessly. *"The Sound Of Music,"* she said. "Unless you can sing the score, you can't rag on me."

He opened his mouth then shut it. "I would have never predicted it."

"Have you ever seen it?"

"Maybe when I was sick with pneumonia in second grade," he said. "I was delirious, so I can't remember."

"Bet you loved it and you just don't want to admit it. Doe, a deer, a female deer," she jokingly sang.

"Ray, a drop of golden sun, and that's enough," he said, taking another sip of beer.

"So you weren't *totally* delirious."

"If I remember that song, then I must have been delirious when I heard it," he said. "You had a fear of the ocean, which we've now solved. Any other fears?"

Only about a hundred, she thought, but couldn't imagine sharing her deepest fear. "Bees," she said. "In particular, wasps."

"Spiders?" he asked.

She shook her head. "Not really. I just smash them."

"A murderer underneath that sweet exterior," he said with a mocking grin.

"When I'm killing a spider, I prefer to think of myself as a mercenary soldier."

He chuckled. "We've worked together for years. Why don't I know any of this?"

"We haven't talked about personal stuff that much until lately. And we've never done anything fun together," she said then winced. "Well, except for work. Work can be fun," she said, quickly correcting herself.

"You're making me sound like a guy who doesn't like to have fun."

"Your work is your fun."

He grimaced then skimmed his finger over her arm, sending a shiver of awareness through her. "Goose bumps," he said. "Are you cold?"

"A little chilly," she confessed. "The sun went behind a cloud and since *someone* insisted that I get drenched…"

"Okay, okay. I'll take you to dinner as penance." He pulled on his shirt.

"Not necessary," she said, reluctantly pulling on her cover-up, wishing the time at the beach hadn't ended so quickly. "I wouldn't want you to feel obligated."

"Not obligated. I want to do it. C'mon," he said and grabbed her hand.

Sophie couldn't remember when Max had touched her so frequently, but maybe she had steeled herself against her attraction to him so that she didn't focus on it. She was aware of his closeness in his car as he drove them back into town. Sophie couldn't imagine ever being able to ignore those football shoulders. His physical strength wasn't her primary attraction to Max, but it sure didn't hurt. His strong personality and generosity had bowled her over since the first day she'd met him. She'd hoped she would become immune to that combination, but it had never happened.

Max let her off outside her apartment. "When can I pick you up?"

"An hour," she said. "I want a hot shower after the cold ocean."

"Never knew you were such a—"

She lifted her hand. "Don't even go there."

"Okay, an hour. Where do you want to eat?"

"Choose some place nice without a wait," she said.

"Nice," he said.

"I could go for some seafood," she suggested.

He nodded. "Sixty minutes and counting."

Sophie dashed out of the car and ran up the stairs to her apartment. Stripping, she stepped into a hot shower she didn't want to leave. But she forced herself, dried off and pulled on a knockabout dress.

Dabbing on a bit of blush, lip gloss and mascara, she ran her fingers through her hair and pulled it up into a messy bun. She grabbed a sweater and suddenly, her phone rang. She glanced at the screen. "You're here already?" she asked.

"I got bored," Max said.

"No surprise there," she said dryly.

"You ready?"

"Close enough," she said. "I'll be downstairs in a couple of moments."

Sophie skipped down the stairs to the front door to find Max waiting for her. She dashed inside the car before he could help her inside.

"You could have let me pretend to be a gentleman," he grumbled, putting the car in gear.

"I saw the cars waiting behind you. Where are we going?"

He smiled. "It's a surprise. Bet you haven't been there."

She felt a ripple of excitement inside her. "I guess I'll find out soon enough."

"You will," he said and turned on some jazz music.

She immediately sank back into her seat and tried not to smell his clean, masculine scent. There was already too much about him that she found irresistible. He drove the car up a winding mountain road and finally stopped outside a restaurant surrounded by lights.

"Ready?" he asked.

"I guess. What's this?"

"The Chantaine Mountain Restaurant," he said. "Spectacular views."

Sophie glanced at her simple beach dress. "Am I appropriately dressed?"

"You're perfect," he said and stepped out of the car. He crossed to her side as she opened the car door. He held the door open and helped her out of the car.

"You're sure about this?" she asked as they walked toward the restaurant.

"Sure as can be," he said and led her inside the front door. He gave his name to the host and they were quickly led to a table next to the windows that surrounded the restaurant.

Sophie sank into her seat, looking down at the beautiful sight below her. Lights shone throughout the mountain beneath them. In the bay, more lights flickered near the water. "It's so lovely."

"Yeah," he said. "Not bad."

She glanced up at him in disbelief. "Not bad? It's stunning."

Max shrugged. "I think what I'm looking at right now is stunning."

Sophie's heart stopped as she realized he was talking about *her*. Reality quickly slapped her upside the head. "Me, stunning? What have you been smoking?" she asked and opened the menu. "You must want me to go to a location where I could get shot or eaten by pygmies."

Chapter Eight

That was when Max realized that seducing Sophie might not be as easy as he'd thought. He was clearly going to have to prove to her that he wanted her. After dinner, he drove back to town and insisted on escorting her to her apartment.

"Thanks for dinner," she said. "It was a fun day."

"Yes, it was," he said and lowered his head toward hers.

He heard her gasp of surprise just before his mouth connected with her ear. She had turned her head.

"What are you doing?" she demanded, clearly peeved. "Do you think I don't remember the last time you did this? And then *apologized?*" She narrowed her eyes at him. "Fool me once, shame on you. Fool me twice, shame on me." She gave a sharp nod of her head. "So, good night," she said and rushed inside her apartment, closing the door in his face.

Scrubbing his chin, he walked down the stairs to his car. *Why had he suddenly decided that he had to have Sophie?* He'd spent years telling himself to stay away from women who he could develop feelings for. Especially her. It would ruin their work relationship. The truth was that the work relationship wasn't enough for him anymore. Not after he'd seen her light up from David's attention. If any man was going to make Sophie smile or laugh, it was going to be him. Not some advisor to Stefan. His desire for her was beginning to feel more like a need. And that could be dangerous.

The following week, Sophie was slammed with work demands. She went in early and stayed late and told herself not to think about how Max had tried to kiss her. The good part of all that work was that she had a valid reason to turn down David the two times he called to ask her out for dinner. When Friday arrived, she was ready to sequester herself in her apartment with some of Chantaine's fabulous gelato and catch some mind-numbing television.

Just as she was leaving the work trailer, Max was walking into it.

"Hey," he said. "Do you have plans tonight?"

"Kinda," she said, trying to scoot past him.

"What are they?" he asked with no apology for his nosiness.

"To be a bum. I'm tired," she said.

"Me, too. Can I be a bum with you?"

She couldn't help smiling. "I don't think you'd like the menu or the itinerary. I'm eating gelato and watching a chick program on television."

"All negotiable," he said. "I'll bring beer and pizza to have before the gelato. Granted, Chantaine pizza is sissy pizza, but we'll make do."

"What about the TV show?"

"We'll figure it out," he hedged, taking off his construction hat.

"I'm not watching *Robocop*," she warned him.

"We'll work it out," he said and stepped into the trailer.

"Should've said I had a date," she muttered to herself. "Would've had a date if I'd said yes to David."

Shrugging off her self-castigation, she got into her car and figured she'd better buy some extra gelato. After she arrived at her apartment, she took a shower and changed into non-seductive, comfy clothes. Jeans and a T-shirt. Perfect, she thought. She was going to pretend that having Max over for a bum night was the same as having a girlfriend visit for a girls' night.

Still suspicious that Max was getting ready to sweet-talk her into the next project, she reached for her mascara. Then she realized what she was doing and jammed the tube back into the cosmetics case.

She ruffled her fingers through her hair and went to the den. She should find the most girly TV show possible. That would make him leave early. Maybe that way she wouldn't make a fool of herself with him again.

Unfortunately, Chantaine didn't carry *Say Yes to yhe Dress*. There was, however, a British period movie on tap. Surely, that would work.

Despite the fact that he was worn out from the work week, Max took the steps to Sophie's apartment two at a time. Juggling beer and a pizza, he realized he'd missed being with just her since last weekend. Even when she was putting him off, she made him feel better inside. He knocked at her door and she took her time answering.

"Hi, there. Listen, I need to warn you that I'm going to have to call an early night tonight. Remember, we're starting work on that center for handicapped kids in the morning, and I'm going to need some rest."

"No problem," he told her, setting the pizza box down on the table. "What are we watching tonight?" he asked, glancing at the television.

"A British period piece," she said with a hint of a cat-like smile. "PBS special. Four hours long."

"Wow," he said, wondering how he would make it through. "I guess we can play drinking games."

"I've never done that and I don't plan—"

"Great time to start," he said, clapping his hands together. "Hey, it's just beer, and you said you needed a good night of sleep."

She rolled her eyes. "I'll get some plates."

Soon enough, she returned with plates and glasses filled with water. "What's with the water?"

"To counter the drinking games," she said, plopping down beside him on the sofa.

"We'll start with FUBAR," he said, putting several bottles of beer on the table. "You got a deck of cards?"

"I'm not sure this is a good idea."

"It's a great idea," he insisted.

Sophie reluctantly got a deck of cards and gave it to him. "What exactly is the game of FUBAR?"

"I shuffle the cards and spread them out on the table. You turn one over and that determines what you drink. Ace you take one drink. You can drink water. I'm not trying to get you drunk."

"I'm not sure about this," she said.

"It'll be fine," he said. "Just fine." He shuffled the cards twice and spread them out on the coffee table. He glanced at her with a sexy smile. "Pick a card."

She did and it was five.

"Five drinks, darlin'," he said and gave her a beer.

Sophie wasn't a fan of drinking games, but she took the sips. "Your turn," she said and leaned back against the sofa.

He drew an eight. "You have to rhyme my word. Weather."

"Heather," she immediately said.

"You're good," he said. "Your draw with the cards."

She pulled a ten of spades.

"Social. Everyone drinks," he said.

She took a baby sip. "If you say so." She also took a sip of water. "Can we take a break and eat pizza?"

"Works for me," he said.

Even though Max called it sissy pizza, Sophie enjoyed it. The pizza seemed a bit more healthy than the North

American counterpart. "Very good," she said. "I wish we could find this in D.C."

"Philadelphia pizza is better," he said.

"That's a matter of opinion," she countered and took another slice of pizza. "I need to pace myself for the gelato."

"We call that ice cream in Ohio," he said, gobbling down a slice of pizza.

"It's better than ice cream," she said as she headed for her freezer. She pulled out the gelato and grabbed some spoons from the drawer and bowls from the cabinet. Returning to the den, she set the carton on the table. "Better than beer. Better than pizza," she said and plunged a large spoon into the gelato.

"If you say so," he said, with a doubtful expression. He scooped a healthy amount into a bowl and lifted a spoonful to his mouth. "It's pretty good."

"It's heavenly," she countered and scooped some into her own bowl. She took a bite and couldn't withhold a moan. "Delicious."

"Yeah," he said, staring at her mouth. "I get it."

"So, you'll never argue with me about gelato again," she said.

"Never," he said, putting his spoon in her bowl and lifting it to her mouth. "Take a bite, sweetheart."

It felt like a bad-girl moment, but Sophie took the gelato in her mouth and licked the bottom of the spoon. She could have sworn she heard him moan when she licked that spoon, but she wasn't sure. Meeting his gaze, she sighed. "Gelato is amazing, isn't it?"

"Yeah," he said. "Let's go back to the card game."

"As long as I can drink water," she said.

"No problem," he said. "Just pick a card."

"Two," she said as she turned over the card.

"You got off easy. Just two drinks."

Sophie took two sips of water.

They continued to play and Sophie alternately drank water and beer. Soon enough, however, she grew drowsy, more from a full, satisfied tummy and the long work week than the measly beer and a half she'd consumed. "Whew, I'm getting tired. Maybe I should go to bed."

"Let me give you a neck massage," he offered. "I hear I'm good at it."

"I bet you are," she said, wondering how many women had complimented his massages, but she turned her back toward him despite her reservations.

Soon enough, he was rubbing her neck and it felt so good. Then she felt him rubbing her back. Then back to her neck again.

"That feels so good," she murmured.

"Yeah," he said, sliding his hands down the side of her breasts and rib cage.

"Ooh," she said. He lifted his hands to her neck and he felt her body melt beneath his fingers. He hoped to get a kiss from her tonight. Maybe more. A surge of arousal slid through him.

"How does this feel?" he asked as he lowered his mouth against her ear.

"Great," she whispered. "Great."

He continued to knead her neck and shoulders, thinking about all the things he wanted to do to her. How much he wanted to kiss her. He could feel how good it would be between them.

He heard a soft strange noise and stopped, lowering his ear so he could hear her better. After several moments, Max realized that Sophie had fallen asleep. She was, in fact, snoring.

Well, hell, Max thought, sighing. No night of passion in his future.

He stared at her for a long moment and felt a warm sensation in his chest. She looked kinda sweet when she was sleeping. He gently picked her up and carried her down the hall to her bedroom.

She frowned and her eyes fluttered as he set her down on the bed. "What—"

"Shh. Sweet dreams," he whispered and brushed a kiss on her head.

He must have reassured her or she was flat-out exhausted because she took a deep breath and fell right back to sleep. Max watched her for a long moment then left her bedroom and cleaned up the trash from the den. He felt oddly reluctant to leave and couldn't explain it for the life of him, but being with Sophie even when she was sleeping felt better than not being with her at all.

Weird, he thought, and dismissed the intimate feelings he had toward her. Must have been that combination of pizza and gelato, he decided and headed to his own apartment.

Sophie awakened to a sliver of light shining through the blinds. Disoriented, she quickly realized that she was in her own bed, but she was wearing jeans and a T-shirt instead of pajamas. The last thing she remembered was getting a wonderful massage from Max. She blinked and sat up. He must have carried her to bed. Embarrassment rushed through her. She must have been far more tired than she'd realized.

Rubbing her sleepiness from her eyes, she glanced at the alarm clock and felt a little shock. Eight o'clock. She would be late for the workday at the center for handicapped children.

She rushed out of bed and took a quick shower, brushed her teeth, dressed, put her hair in a ponytail and grabbed a granola bar as she headed for the door. Something about the den nagged at her and she turned around. The cards were neatly stacked on the table and all signs of pizza, beer and gelato were out of sight. Curious, she returned to the kitchen to find a clean empty sink and dishes drying on the rack.

Her heart softened. He'd cleaned up before he left. How sweet was that? How was she supposed to resist him now?

Catching sight of the kitchen clock kicked her back into gear. She needed to get moving to get to the project center. She found a parking space for her car on a side street then rushed inside the building, which was full of activity. She saw Terri and her husband, Bob, pulling the frame from a doorway. Terri glanced up. "We're in the destruction phase. Tear it down before you rebuild."

Sophie smiled. She was all too familiar with demolition. She'd been on several projects where it had been necessary to get rid of faulty construction before starting new. "You always did enjoy that part of a project."

"How often can you tear up something and get praised for it?" Terri asked.

"So true," Sophie said and glanced around the room. "Have you seen—" She broke off when she spotted Max wearing her favorite style. Low-slung jeans and a T-shirt stretched tight across his wide shoulders, he had also tied a handkerchief around his head as a sweatband. Total male and total physical. He looked at her and her stomach dipped.

His lips lifted in a slow grin and he waved at her.

Her heart fluttering all over itself, Sophie told herself to calm down. *It's just Max.* She took a deep breath and walked toward him.

"How are you, sleepyhead?" he asked with a sexy smile.

She felt her cheeks heat with self-consciousness. "Sorry I fell asleep on you. I was obviously much more tired than I'd thought."

"No problem. You've got a cute little snore," he said.

Horrified, she stared at him. "Oh, tell me that's not true. I do *not* snore."

"Don't worry about it. It's not like you sounded like a truck driver."

She cringed with embarrassment. "Well." She cleared her throat. "I'm here. What can I do to help?"

"We've got most of the demolition tasks covered in

here. Do you mind doing some work outside? It'll be mostly pulling weeds. Did you bring gloves?"

She shook her head.

"I've got some extra. Thanks for coming. You don't have to stay all day," he said.

"I think I'm caught up on my rest," she said.

Sophie enjoyed working outside. The sun was shining, the temperature was perfect and a slight breeze kept her from getting too warm. After she pulled weeds, she progressed to loading broken granite into a wheelbarrow and toting it to the truck that would haul it away.

"Oh, my goodness, I can't believe this. He's made a slave of you," Princess Bridget's voice called from behind Sophie. She shot Sophie a look of unadulterated horror. "What are you doing?"

Sophie smiled. "Helping?"

Bridget sputtered. "Not this way. You shouldn't be doing hard labor like this," she said.

As usual, Bridget was dressed like a peacock. Head-to-toe green today with a green hat and green heels.

"Lovely to see you, your highness. It's not bad. I've enjoyed being outside, getting some physical activity. It's a nice break from being cooped up in the office trailer."

"I suppose being outside would be nice, but this is going too far," she insisted.

"I really don't mind," Sophie said. "What brings you here? I'm sure you didn't pop by just to scold me for pulling weeds."

"No, of course not," Bridget said. "I wanted to tell my half brother, the slave driver, that I've made arrangements for the charity event. We're going to have a night of gambling, with the proceeds going to fund the center for handicapped children. Doesn't that sound like fun? You could go with David," she suggested. "And, of course you'll need a new dress."

"Whoa," Sophie said. "One thing at a time. I was surprised we were able to get started on this before the charity event."

"I was, too," Bridget said. "But my brother-in-law Nic found this building and was able to lease it for a song. Max said an anonymous donor had put up an initial investment. I must say the community will gladly support this once it gets started. The people of Chantaine are very compassionate and generous."

"They have a pretty good example from the Devereauxes," Sophie said.

Bridget smiled. "That was a lovely thing to say. Speaking of your being so lovely, Pippa is wishing for some girl time. Perhaps we can lunch soon?"

"I don't know. Things have been very busy at the work site. Max has to make as much progress as possible when all the machinery is working and the materials are available."

"I suppose," Bridget said. "Perhaps next Saturday. You'll be off then, won't you?"

"Unless I'm working here."

"Not if I have anything to say about it," she said indignantly. "Hauling broken concrete. Of all things," she said. "Is Maxwell inside? Would you like to join me while I tell him the charity plans?"

Sophie lifted her gloved hands and wiggled her fingers. "Oh, I'll let you take it from here," she said.

"Very well," Bridget said. "But we're on for lunch next Saturday. Ciao," she said as she walked into the building.

"Ouch," Sophie whispered, hoping Bridget wasn't going to fuss at Max too much. After all, he was doing something good for her country. Sophie hauled a few more loads of broken concrete and called it good. Her back was tired and she was ready for a shower. She decided not to sign off with Max. It was too dangerous to be alone with him.

Sophie grabbed a salad from a café just before it closed and headed to her apartment. Shoving the salad into the fridge, she stripped off her clothes and headed straight for the shower. The hot spray fell over her and she willed it to wash thoughts of Max from her mind.

After her shower, she pulled on comfy jammies and sank into her couch to watch some mindless television. She flipped through several channels and settled on a BBC contemporary comedy. She needed the subtitles to get all the jokes, but who had to know? Laughing at the British humor, she heard a knock at her door.

Sophie rose from the sofa to look through her peephole. Max was still dressed in his manly man clothes and bandana headband. She briefly considered not opening the door, but he banged on it again.

Sophie opened the door. "Hello?"

"How the hell could you leave me with Bridget?

She tore a strip off of me because I let you do physical labor?"

"I tried to tell her I enjoyed being outside," she said.

"She didn't believe it."

"Is that why you're here?" she asked.

"Not really," he said and walked through the door. "I know you have leftover pizza in your fridge. I put it there."

"What if I already ate it?" she asked as she headed for her teeny galley kitchen.

He glanced over his shoulder, pinning her with his gaze. "Did you?"

She paused. "No," she confessed.

"Like I said," he muttered and within seconds, he brought the cold pizza with him as he paced the den. "Can't believe that woman," he said. "She told me I was a slave driver. A slave driver," he said in disbelief. "Not onc of my employees would say that about me."

"Well," Sophie said.

He shot her a hard look. "Well?"

"Well, you do expect a lot of your employees," she said. "Especially during crunch time."

"But I'm no slave driver," he demanded.

She chewed her lip.

Max swallowed a cold bite of pizza and swore. "Why didn't you tell me?"

"It's all relative," she said. "Everyone understands the need for overtime. If they don't die from it," she said in a lower voice.

He swore again.

"You're intense," Sophie said, rising from the sofa. "Not everyone can deal with that. But you do give them freedom to leave if it's too much for them."

"Why don't I feel better?" he asked, inhaling the last of his pizza slice.

"Bridget is the female you," she said.

His face fell and he nearly choked. "Bridget is me?"

"The female you," she corrected. "She's a high achiever in her own way. She pushes people to do what she wants them to do. She may be the Devereaux most like you."

He stared at her for a long moment. "I can't remember when I've been more insulted."

Sophie laughed under her breath. "It's the curse of the high achiever," she teased.

He groaned and shook his head. "Or not," he said and returned the rest of the pizza to her fridge. He disappeared for a moment then returned with a determined, seductive look in his gaze.

Her stomach took a crazy dip.

"I need a shower," he said, pulling off his makeshift headband. "Wanna join me?"

Her heart stopped in her throat. "I—uh, already took a shower," she managed.

"So?" he said.

A thousand questions filled her mind. A thousand doubts rolled through her. "Uh, the towels are under the sink."

"Okay," he said and pulled off his shirt and left it on the floor. His jeans followed. She shouldn't have looked, but she saw when his boxers hit the floor. Max had a great…body.

Sophie paced the den. She'd just been issued the sexiest invitation of her life. She'd wanted Max *for as long as she could remember*. What if she accepted? What if she turned him down? Would she regret it forever?

Her heart felt as if it was lodged in her throat. *Oh, please,* she thought. *Help me make the right decision*. In her next breath, she knew. There was no choice. There was only Max.

Stripping off her clothes, she made her way to the bathroom. The steam from the shower permeated the small room. Taking her heart in her hand, she pulled back the shower curtain and stepped into the tub.

Max looked down at her for a long, breath-taking moment then pulled her against him and took her mouth. A cacophony of sensations raced through her. Warm water, hard muscles, soft sensual lips.

His hands skimmed over her shoulders then down her waist to her hips. He drew her against him, brushing his mouth from side to side against hers. Sophie's heart was beating so fast she could hardly breathe. He squeezed her buttocks and slid his thigh between hers. He lifted one of his hands to one of her breasts. Dipping his mouth to her shoulder, he licked at her wet skin. His hand slid between her legs and he found all her secret sensitive places. She clung to him as he took turns with each of her nipples, drawing them into his mouth.

She was so turned on she could hardly breathe.

Max lifted his head. "I want you too much," he muttered against her mouth.

With the warm shower raining down on them, he pushed her against the wall of the shower and took her, and Sophie knew she would never be the same.

Chapter Nine

Somehow, they ended up in her bed. He pulled her against him.

Sophie was caught between total happiness and terror.

"You okay?" Max asked.

"Sure," she managed, but her heart hadn't stopped racing. She hoped she didn't go into cardiac arrest.

"You don't sound okay," he said, pulling back to look at her.

"I'm fine. I just don't take a shower with—someone like you every night," she said.

He met her gaze and his mouth lifted in a half smile. "That's good to know."

She laughed, half out of hysteria, half from relief and buried her head against his chest. "You are not an easy man, Max," she said.

"Hey, I was pretty easy for you. Took my clothes off and invited you into your shower. How much easier could I get?"

Try issuing that invitation two years ago, she thought. She took a deep breath. "So is this a one-night stand? I'd like to be prepared," she said.

He slid his thigh between her legs and lowered his mouth. "Not if I have anything to do with it."

So they become lovers. Secret lovers. Max didn't appear to want to let anyone know that they were involved and frankly neither did she. What if it ended in one week? Or two? She couldn't help feeling on edge. She didn't want to have to make explanations. Maybe Max didn't either.

Just as soon as her doubts overwhelmed her, on Wednesday he visited her at her apartment and they shared an evening where they played a card game, built a free-form LEGO creation and then he made love to her.

She made it through the week and was relieved when Friday arrived. No more pretending and trying to fake it in front of Terri and the others in the office.

She took a shower and put on her yoga pants and a tank, suspecting that she might hear a knock on her door any moment. Just as she considered dialing for delivery, a knock sounded on the door. Her heart lifted and she couldn't help smiling.

She opened the door. "Hello?"

"Hello, darlin'," he said, setting the pizza package

and beer on her sofa table. He picked her up and swung her around. "I brought pizza and beer."

She swallowed a laugh. "And what if I wanted champagne and gourmet food?" she asked.

"Then I would get it for you," he said solemnly. "Tomorrow. Because I want to keep you busy in bed tonight."

Her laugh burst through her restraint. "If you say so," she said. "I'm having lunch with Princess Bridget and Pippa tomorrow. They insisted and they've been so kind to me I feel I must accept."

He lifted a dark eyebrow as he let her slide down his body. "Bridget is a pushy girl. Be careful."

"She has a good heart," she said.

"She introduced you to that David guy," he said with a frown.

"He was very nice," she countered.

Max scowled. "I did not like him."

"He kinda made you realize you wanted me," she said.

"True," Max said. "But you still need to be careful about her. She may try to match you up with someone else."

She shrugged. "Unless I'm taken."

He met her gaze and lowered his eyes. "I do my best to take you every chance I get."

She couldn't resist laughing at his possessive gaze and growl. "I want to do something interesting tomorrow night," she said.

"We do something interesting every night we're together."

"I want you to surprise me."

He looked at her for a moment. "Okay, but no pro-tests."

She realized she shouldn't have put out such a gen-eral request. "Uh—"

"No protests," he said.

She closed her eyes, saying a little prayer. "Okay, no protests."

"Good," he said. "Pizza and beer and you in bed. Per-fect Friday night."

She couldn't deny it was a perfect night. Just Max and her together the whole night. Laughter, kisses and lovemaking. He was gone before she awakened the next morning and she felt a little guilty that she wasn't help-ing with the charity project, but she fell back asleep for a while.

Sophie dragged herself out of bed, took a shower and put on a shirtdress she'd bought a couple years ago. Thank goodness her mother had encouraged her to make a few timeless clothing purchases. Stepping into a pair of low pumps, she worked fruitlessly with her hair and applied mascara and lip gloss.

Staring in the mirror, Sophie decided this was as good as she was going to get today. Better than most days. Soon enough, it was time for her to meet the princesses at an exclusive café. Battling Bridget's insistence that Sophie should accept a ride from the palace, Sophie drove herself and parked two blocks away.

She walked inside the café and gave her name to the hostess.

"I will take you to your table," she said and led her to a private room in the back of the building.

Moments later, she was served a glass of water and a cup of hot tea just before Bridget and Pippa arrived with the baby in an infant seat.

"Sorry we're late," Pippa said. "Amelie wanted to nurse at the last moment, but she should be good for a while."

Sophie glanced into the infant carrier at the sleeping baby. She looked completely relaxed. "What a sweetie."

"Most of the time," Pippa said with a smile. "I'm so glad to be out and about lunching with you and Bridget."

"Of course you are," Bridget said, pulling her hat from her head. "Heavens, what a morning. The cattle tried to trample the boys. The chickens were screaming at dawn. I just want to sleep in one morning each week. Is that too much to ask?" She waved to the waitress. "A glass of pinot grigio, please. For all of us."

"I'll sip," Pippa said.

"I don't usually drink before evening," Sophie said and saw Bridget's lifted eyebrow. "But I can make an exception."

Bridget's mouth lifted in a smile. "What a week it's been. You'll be happy to hear that the invitations for the charity gambling event have been sent and I've already received a ton of replies from those who want to attend. Good news."

Sophie nodded. "That is good news. You've done an amazing job in such a short time."

Bridget shrugged. "It's what I do. That said, Pippa has pulled off a major coup."

Pippa rocked her baby's infant seat on the table. "I'm sure it was a collaborative effort."

"She's being too humble," Bridget said. "Pippa has accomplished an amazing feat. She has persuaded The Royal Society for a Better World to meet in Chantaine next year with an option to continue to meet here for an additional two years."

Sophie blinked. "Sorry. I'm not familiar with that Society. Is it a fraternity?"

"The Royal Society is centuries old. Royals meet at the conference to find ways to make the world a better place," Pippa said. She smiled sheepishly. "What can I say? They want to come to our beaches."

"It's more than that," Bridget said. "They were influenced by you, Pippa."

"You're embarrassing me," Pippa shyly said and took a sip of her water.

"You deserve the credit," Bridget insisted.

"Can we change the subject please?" Pippa asked.

Bridget shrugged. "I suppose." She frowned and turned in Sophie's direction. "What's going on with David?"

Sophie tensed, but decided she should keep Bridget straight. "I just want to be friends with David. I told him this week. He's a wonderful man, but I just want to be friends with him."

"Well, darn," she said. "I was so sure about him. He's

both Italian and German. Charming and practical. As perfect as it gets."

Sophie nodded. "Yes, but you can't plan chemistry."

"Bet he had plenty for you," Bridget grumbled. "Oh, well, I may find another."

"Please don't," Sophie said. "I'm happy the way I am."

Bridget smiled. "We can always be happier."

Heaven help her, Sophie thought. Pippa exchanged a knowing glance with her.

After lunch with the Devereauxes, she returned to her apartment and wasn't sure what to do with herself. She considered going out, but decided to wait. Soon enough, a knock sounded on her door.

She opened it and Max stood there wearing a pair of sweatpants and a sweatshirt. "Put on your swimsuit, girl."

"It's going to be cold," she said.

"I'll keep you warm," he promised.

"I'm going to freeze," she said because she knew it was true. If it had been cold in the early afternoon the other day, then it would feel like ice cubes at the late time of day.

"I promise you that you won't stay cold very long," he said.

"If I die in that ocean, it's your fault."

"What are you bellyachin' about? You've got plenty of life insurance," he said.

Sophie rolled her eyes and went to her bedroom to put on her bathing suit and a pair of jeans and a sweater. She grabbed her towel, stepped into a pair of flip-flops and braced herself. "Ready for action," she said as she entered the den.

"You make me want to forget the whole plan and just take you to bed," he said.

"Well, darn, you've already dared me," she said.

"Then we're going to a secret place," he said and grabbed her hand. He led her down the stairway to his car, ushered her inside and drove away from town.

"Which beach are we visiting?" she asked.

"I didn't say we were going to a beach," he said. "We're going to a place that will accommodate us," he said in a mysterious voice that worried her a little. Was he talking about a nude beach?

"Excuse me?"

"We're going to a place that will accommodate us," he repeated.

"What does that mean?"

"It's a surprise. I've told you all I'm going to tell you. You'll just have to wait and see," he said and turned his car stereo system to jazz music.

Both eager and nervous to see what he had planned, she kept waiting for him to turn toward the beach. Instead he headed up the winding road of a mountain. "Where on earth—" she muttered as he pulled onto yet another road.

One more turn and they were on a dirt road that led to a small chalet in a clearing. "Well, this is interesting. Who lives here?" she asked.

"One of the local construction company owners I've met. Turns out, he has a child who is handicapped, so he's excited about our project. He owns several homes on the island. This is one of the most unique because of its location, the view and the springs behind it." He got out of the car and jogged to her side to help her out of her seat.

"Springs? Is that why I need my bathing suit?" she asked, growing more curious with each step they took. The moonlight shone over the house, but the area just beyond was covered with trees.

The walkway behind the home was lit with in-ground lighting. She followed Max down the hill and heard the sound of running water. "Bet it's freezing."

"But look at the view," he said.

She couldn't deny how beautiful it was. With the stars overhead and the ocean below, the setting was almost mystical. "You go first."

"Okay, but you have to promise to come in right after I go," he said.

"I promise," she said.

Max stripped down to his bathing suit and put his foot in the water. He gave an audible gasp.

Great. It was worse than she'd thought.

He stepped down the stone steps into the spring, swearing and making terrifying noises. He turned to face her, huddling his arms around his chest, his teeth chattering. "Your turn," he said.

Sophie considered running in the opposite direction, but a deal was a deal. Plus, he would never let her live it down if she didn't follow through.

"What's taking so long?" he asked.

"Okay, okay," she said. "I'm coming." Stripping off the clothes that covered her bathing suit, she placed her towel close to the edge of the springs. Bracing herself, took her first step.

The water was warm, almost hot. She gaped at Max in surprise. "You liar," she said. "This isn't at all cold. Shame on you for teasing me."

He gave a belly laugh. "I couldn't resist. Doesn't it feel great?"

She stepped the rest of the way into the bubbling pool, her body relaxing under the warm water. "Wonderful," she said. "How did you find out about this?"

"I was shooting the breeze with the construction owner and he mentioned it. This place is usually rented, but not this weekend, so he told me I could enjoy it for the evening. And you were expecting a nude beach," he said. "Admit it."

"Well," she said. "Do you blame me?"

"I'm more creative than that. You can't get much better than this. Nature's Jacuzzi," he said and pulled her against him. "You like it?"

Enjoying the sensation of his arms around her and his strong body against hers, she nodded. "How could I not like it?"

"Good," he said. "I might be able to outdo Stefan's Mr. Perfect economic advisor."

"I didn't know there was a competition," she said.

"You're right. There wasn't." He slid his mouth over her neck and ripples of pleasure washed over her, but his reference to David niggled at her.

She turned to look at him. "Is that the only reason you suddenly decided you wanted me? Because of David?"

Max shook his head. "No."

"Well it sure seems like it. I get attention from one guy, then all of a sudden you see me as more than a handy assistant."

Max sighed. "What got to me was how happy you looked. I wanted to be the one to make you happy."

Her heart melted. She lifted her hand to his hard jaw in wonder. "Wow," she said and smiled.

"Wow is what I say about you," he said and picked her up and twirled her around in the water. He took her mouth in a delicious kiss that sent her mind and body spinning. The kiss turned more passionate when he pulled her against him where he was hard and wanting her.

"I want you," he said and she felt him untie the top of her bathing suit and push it to her waist.

Forbidden desire rushed through her. She was topless in the warm, rippling spring with Max. Why didn't she feel more self-conscious?

His chest strong and hard against hers, she felt herself sinking under his spell. He pushed her bathing suit all the way down her legs and she reveled in the sensation of her bare skin against his. He caressed and played with her in all the right places, making her want more.

Finally, he propped against the stone wall of the spring and pulled her down over him. He thrust intimately inside her as she locked herself around his hips. The heat in his hooded eyes did something to her, and the sensation of him moving and stretching inside her took her over the top. She cried out and he covered her mouth with kisses. Within a heartbeat, he stiffened and thrust inside her with one last powerful stroke, and she felt completely one with him.

Max enjoyed his moments with Sophie, but he couldn't escape the pressures of work and the commitment he'd made to build the center for handicapped children. When Sunday night hit, he was already thinking about Monday, Tuesday and every day after. He was getting pressure from headquarters to wrap up the Chantaine road construction and everyone had underestimated how much longer it took to get anything done on an island. His supervisor wasn't at all happy. Max was inclined to give him a piece of his mind, but the company was comping a *lot* of the cost of this job, so he had to mute himself, which made him cranky.

The Devereauxes had invited him to one event after another ever since he had arrived, but he had turned down most of the invites. He still didn't feel close to his so-called family and wasn't sure if he wanted to get involved with them. He was much more comfortable helping them then withdrawing.

After four fifteen-hour days, Sophie stepped in front of him before he could make it to his desk in the trailer. "Hey, where's the fire?"

"Under my butt to get this done," he said. "What do you want?"

Her eyes grew wide. "Whoa," she said softly. "Bridget

has called me three times today because you're not re-turning her calls."

"I don't have time to talk to the princess," he snapped and moved to step around her.

"She wants to know if you have any names you want to add to the address list for invitations to the charity event. It's the week after next," she said.

"Oh," he said, slowing down and thinking. "I have a few. I'll send them to her through email."

"When?" Sophie asked.

He turned around and tilted his head at her. "When?"

"Yes," Sophie said. "She needed them yesterday. Since she's contributing her connections to this event, you need to cooperate."

He groaned. "I know," he said. "These events just aren't my thing. I'd never make it as a royal. I like to get things *done*."

"They get things done, just in their way," she said. "And she is helping us with this."

"Okay, names by tomorrow," he said, sinking into his chair.

"Are you okay?" she asked. "I'm concerned about you."

"Regular deadline crunch. Headquarters is screaming at me. I knew it would be tough getting what we need on an island, but not this tough," he said, staring at his computer screen.

"Is there something I can do?" she asked.

Her question caught him off guard, even though she'd asked him the same question a dozen other times. Something in his heart twisted, and he looked up at her. Same Sophie. His amazing assistant, and now his lover. He'd complicated their relationship, but he couldn't regret it. Maybe sometime down the road, but not now.

"Just be you," he said.

"Sounds pretty lame and not all that helpful," she said with a wry smile.

He rose from his desk and dropped a sweet, but brief kiss on her lips. "Trust me. You're making this livable." He winked and returned to his desk. "Save Friday night for me. I may not be worth much then, but I'd like to spend the evening with you."

She lifted her hand to his face. "I think I can manage that," she said and a shot of warm relief spread throughout him. The feeling was a little too strong for his comfort.

On Friday, Max took lunch with his construction friend Aloisius Janton. The two men ate sandwiches at one of Al's job sites. "Hey, I wanted to thank you for letting me visit your house last weekend."

"Why didn't you stay all night?" Al asked. He was a forty-something man with a balding head, a dark tan and furrowed eyebrows. "You could have stayed all weekend."

"Not necessary. The springs were magical enough," Max said.

"My pleasure," Al said. "I'm pleased with your work both in the north end and in the city."

"Speaking of my work in the city, I wanted to let you know that there's going to be a benefit. It's a Monte Carlo gambling kind of thing. Princess Bridget is arranging it," he said and took a bite of his sandwich.

"Her Highness Bridget Devereaux?" Al asked with a surprised gaze.

"Yeah. Princess Bridget. Wanna go?" he asked.

"Of course I do," Al said. "May I bring Jonathan and his mother?"

"Sure," Max said. "But are you sure you want Jonathan to be the poster child for handicapped children from Chantaine?"

Al lifted his chin with pride. "I would be very proud for Jonathan to represent those children who are struggling with handicaps. He has overcome so much."

Surprised by Al's response about Bridget, Max absorbed the man's pride and need. "Then your family will have a front-row seat. I'll make sure of it," he said.

With the sun shining down on them, the two men continued to eat sandwiches. "How's the road coming along?" Al asked.

"I don't see how you do it," Max said. "How do you estimate the date of completion when your materials or equipment come in late?"

Al, with his half-bald head, laughed. "Always add six months. It will make you look good when you complete it before deadline."

"I wish I'd talked to you sooner," Max said.

"You'll do okay," Al said. "Just tell your supers to back off. You can do that. They won't question you. They value you too much, as they should."

"You don't know me that well," Max said. "What makes you say that?"

"You make things happen," Al said. "Your company would be terrified to lose you."

"Hmm," Max said. "I usually thought I was in a position of strength, but I never thought they would be afraid to lose me."

"Look at what you've accomplished during the last few years," Al said. "Who else in your company has done so well?"

"I have no idea," Max replied. "I'm too busy taking care of my own projects."

Al laughed. "You should always check your competition."

"Who has time for that?" Max asked.

"The man who wishes to maximize his income."

"I'll think about that."

"Don't think too long," Al said. "Act."

Max saw that Al was savvy. He extended his hand to him. "You're an impressive man."

"I do the best with what I have. That's my rule in life."

"I never spend much time thinking past next year," Max said. "You've given me a different point of view."

"My point of view changed when Jonathan was born. He was intellectually superior, but physically vulnerable. Changed my whole investing scheme."

"Jonathon is a lucky boy."

"I'm a lucky father," Al corrected.

"I'd like to meet him," Max said. "You've made me curious."

"You shall at the gambling night with Princess Bridget. She is quite the princess," Al said. "Prince Stefan takes heat for his father, but he is a huge improvement over Prince Edward. All of the current royals are very compassionate. That's why I continue to live in Chantaine. The royals are generous and compassionate. What country has harder working royals?"

Max stared at Al for a long moment. "You actually like the Devereauxes?"

"Of course I do. Who wouldn't? They try to improve the economy. They try to improve our lives. What's not to like?"

Max absorbed Al's sentiment and took a long drink of water. "I'll think about that."

Al laughed. "You've already thought about it," Al said. "The reason you are here is because you, too, are intrigued by the Devereauxes. In a way, you are one of them. Take a breath and let that wash over you. You are a Devereaux. A royal. You act like a royal from the way you finish the road that will make Chantaine a better country to the way you build a house for handicapped children. It's in your blood."

"Maybe I'm just a nice guy," Max said.

Al laughed uncontrollably.

After their lunch, Max returned to the worksite. A machine had broken down and Terri's husband helped him fix it. He was going to have to hire Terri's trucker husband, Bob, as a regular if everything continued to break down.

Max and the workers worked until sunset and did the

same the next day. Thank goodness Sophie was in his future at the end of this day. He couldn't wait to see her face and feel her arms around him.

Chapter Ten

On Friday, Max went straight to Sophie's apartment. It was dark by the time he arrived. "Sorry," he apologized as she opened the door. "No hot springs tonight."

"I don't need hot springs every night." She smiled. "Just every now and then."

"Do you mind if I head for the shower?"

"No problem. I've already been there. I have a roasted chicken for dinner."

"Sounds awesome. Even better than pizza," he said.

She laughed. "Go take your shower. I may even let you watch an action movie."

"What did I do to deserve that?" he asked as he headed toward her bathroom.

"You're a good guy," she said. "You just try to hide it."

His stomach clenched at her words. He hoped she didn't count on him too much.

Drowning himself under the shower, he finally shut it off and dried off. He dressed in sweatpants and a T-shirt and was thankful Sophie didn't expect more from him. She knew what he'd gone through during the last week.

He made his way to the den where she served chicken, mashed potatoes and green beans on the sofa table. "I feel like I've died and gone to heaven."

"We all need a comfort meal every now and then," she said.

He spooned the food onto his plate. "You're a rock star. I didn't know you knew how to fix all this."

"My mother was born in the South. Learning to cook this way was a requirement."

"I'm thankful for your requirements," he said and took his first bite of mashed potatoes. "I've just gone to heaven."

Sophie laughed. "You're desperate for comfort food."

"Or I'm desperate for you," he said, meeting her gaze for a long moment before he dug into the food once again.

"Don't charm me too much," she said. "You'll scare me."

"Hey, I'm not tricking you," he said. "You should be able to tell. I'm not asking you to go to Mars for our next project."

"But you haven't said anything about the next project."

"Because I'm still focused on this project," he said,

still intent on enjoying the meal. "Headquarters is riding me to get it done."

"It makes it tough," she said. "You have to race like mad when everything comes together."

He pointed at her and nodded. "Exactly."

"But you're going to have to deal with Bridget about the charity event at some point," she added.

He nodded, taking a breath even though he was still hungry. "I know. By the way, will you come to Bridget's casino night with me?"

She paused. "Yes, but how are you going to explain—" She paused. "Us."

He shrugged. "I don't believe in overexplaining, but if anyone asks, then I'll just say I thought it was appropriate that our company present a united front for this charity."

She met his gaze then looked away. "Oh."

He frowned, hesitating before he took his next bite. "What else should I say?"

"Nothing," she said. "Nothing."

"Do you want other people to know we're involved?" he asked.

She looked into his eyes for a long moment and a thousand emotions swept over her face. "Um. Probably not."

"Exactly. Our relationship is nobody's business but ours."

She gave a slow nod. "So you're not ashamed of us?"

He blinked. *Ashamed.* The word stabbed at him. "No," he said. "I'm not ashamed. It's just nobody else's business. I don't want any comments or suggestions from clowns on the sidelines. We're doing okay on our own."

She faked a smile. "Yeah, we are."

She wanted to believe that the only reason why he hadn't gone public with their relationship was because he's a private person. But she held back tears thinking that he probably didn't believe that the relationship would last, so why tell everyone? She had to face it, with such a beautiful and romantic setting, romance was bound to spring up…then be dismissed upon their leaving.

"I'm glad we're straight on that," he said.

"Go ahead and eat," she murmured. "I'm not going to grill you."

He met her gaze and felt a pinch of pain. "Thanks. I don't want anything to mess up what we have."

She covered his hand with hers. "No worries," she said, referencing the Australian lingo they learned together.

"You're a goddess," he said and continued to eat the delicious meal. He just hoped Sophie wouldn't bail on him when she realized the truth about him. Because eventually, she would. She would see that he was not the kind of man a woman wanted for a long-term relationship, even if he was beginning to want just that.

After he finished eating, he joined her on the sofa with every intention of making love to her. He was going to kiss every inch of her, take her in every possible way. He wanted her so much he could taste her. He relaxed against the back of the sofa. It felt so good to be with her.

His next conscious thought was when Sophie was pulling on his arm. "Max," Sophie said. "You're snoring."

Max shook his head. "I don't snore."

She laughed. "I don't either. Come to bed." She urged him to his feet.

"I'm so sleepy. What time is it?" he asked, looking around for a clock.

"Very late," she said, pushing him toward the bedroom. He took several steps and she nudged him into bed.

"I want to make love to you," he said drowsily, still not fully awake. "I want you."

"Maybe in the morning, cowboy," she whispered with a chuckle in her voice.

"Why are you laughing?" he protested.

"I'm not laughing," she said, stroking his forehead. "Relax. Sleep."

He ached to hold her, but sleep called him, demanding his submission. He fought it, but Sophie's bed was so comfortable and smelled sweet, like her. He couldn't help himself and he drifted away....

Sometime later, he half awakened and felt her sexy slim body next to his. Cotton interfered with the nonstop skin he wanted to feel, but he took a deep breath and her scent lulled him into semiconsciousness.

Hours later, Max reawakened. He felt like an army had trudged through his mouth. Taking a deep breath, he eased himself from the bed and walked to the bathroom to brush his teeth and take a long drink of water.

He splashed some water on his face. It awakened him slightly, but he still felt drowsy.

Returning to bed, he slid under the covers and moved close to Sophie. She shifted and wriggled against him. He pulled her against him and put his hand over her flat belly. She sighed and it vibrated through him.

He immediately grew aroused, but he told himself to calm down. Max knew this was a special moment. He'd been careful not to grow too attached to other women, and he knew it was a mistake this time, too. But he was either too selfish or she had wore down his willpower. As she awakened and lifted her head to him, she reminded him of a flower turning toward the sun. The idea that he could be her sun even for a moment sent a dozen crazy emotions through him. Following his strongest emotion at the moment, he kissed her and made love to her.

"How are things with you and Mister Max?" Terri asked Sophie in a low voice while Max was gone from the work trailer.

"Interesting," Sophie said, unsure of how much she should confide.

"You've finally hooked up," Terri said with certainty, because she was entirely too smart.

Sophie didn't like the term *hooked up*. It cheapened her feelings for Max. At the same time, she couldn't help believing he saw their romantic relationship as temporary. She couldn't forget that eye-opening conversation with him when she'd first arrived in Chantaine. He'd been adamantly opposed to even the idea of a long-term commitment. "I didn't say that," Sophie said, feeling twitchy and nervous.

"You said it with your face and body language," Terri said. "Anything wrong? He's not kinky, is he?"

"No. He's not kinky," Sophie quickly said and took a breath. "But I know he thinks he's not relationship material. He wants to keep things between us on the down low."

"I don't like that," Terri said, her mouth pulling into a firm line.

"I have mixed feelings about it, but I don't want to have to answer a lot of questions about Max and me either," Sophie said.

Terri looked at her for a moment. "I can see that," she said. "My husband was straightforward once he decided I was the one. He didn't care who knew, but Max is a different animal. In the whole time I've known him, he's never announced an attachment to a woman. But I'm betting you're different for him."

Her stomach dipped. "We'll see. He wants me to go to the charity event with him."

"And he thinks that won't cause a stir?" Terri asked.

"He plans to explain it as the company presenting a united front."

"Yeah, good luck with that," Terri said. "Make sure you wear something distracting to make a liar out of him. He deserves that."

Sophie bit her lip. "I only have two dresses appropriate for this."

"Then buy another one," Terri said bluntly.

Thankfully, Max burst into the work trailer, which meant Sophie didn't need to reply.

"I need some figures," he directed toward Sophie.

"I'm ready," she said while noticing his sigh.

"Thanks," he said, relieved. "This is what I need."

Sophie input his requests into her laptop as he spoke. From his request she noticed he was concerned about an increased cost in supplies. She knew that Max was under pressure to keep costs down and finish the job as soon as possible. The big problem with that was that Max didn't believe in cutting corners. He did it right or didn't do it at all, and she respected him for that.

She researched the particular road material that he wanted and wrangled a decent price from the supplier. The only problem was that they couldn't deliver until next week.

Max clenched his jaw and shrugged. "It is what it is. Thanks."

Sophie felt bad for him. She knew he was doing the best he could and wanted to get this done for Chantaine, but it was turning out to be far more difficult than he'd planned.

Later that day, Pippa called and begged Sophie to join her for dinner at the palace. Sophie couldn't possibly refuse the sweet princess. With baby Amelie nearby, Sophie enjoyed a gourmet meal with Pippa.

"This is so nice," Sophie said. "How did you end up at the palace?"

"When my husband, Nic, goes out of the country for

business, he insists I stay at the palace," Pippa said with a sigh. "It's a good thing Amelie doesn't mind going from one place to the next."

"Why does he travel so much?" Sophie asked.

"He would say he's managing his businesses, but I know he's also trying to bring in new business for Chantaine. He's an overachiever, but he insists he will take off the summer to spend with the baby and me."

"Will he do that?" Sophie asked as she took a bite of the delicious puff pastry entrée.

"I believe he will. He's starting to get impatient about leaving Amelie and me," Pippa said with a smile. "It's a bit amusing to watch."

Sophie chuckled. "Good for all of you."

"And has Bridget been trying matchmake anymore?" Pippa asked.

"No. I've dodged that bullet," Sophie said firmly.

"I'm sure Bridget is crushed. She keeps trying to engineer a match, but no luck so far."

"Maybe her efforts are helping more than she thinks. In your case, she tried to match you up with a man you didn't want, and that only intensified the relationship between you and your husband."

"True," Pippa said as she took a bite of the entrée. "But in your case, she has utterly failed."

"Not necessarily," Sophie said. "Sometimes a date with a man can help you define what you really want."

Pippa nodded. "Very true. You're a wise woman. What do you want?"

"Probably something I can't have forever, but I'm okay with that."

Pippa grimaced. "That's terrible."

"And you never felt that way about your husband before you were married?"

Pippa hesitated. "You make an excellent point. We're all on a journey," she said. "Always. Even Fredericka is having a hard time."

"Fredericka?" Sophie echoed. "She's one of your sisters."

"Yes," Pippa said. "I shouldn't have mentioned it, but I feel I can trust you. Apparently her marriage is in trouble. We're all worried about her."

"I'm so sorry," Sophie said. "I hope things will turn around for her."

"We do, too. Years ago, Fredericka had addiction issues. If she has marriage problems, we fear she may return to her bad habits."

"I hope not," Sophie said, empathizing with Pippa's concern. "Do you think she needs a visit from one of her sisters?"

"She refuses a visit. All of us have offered. Valentina, who lives in the States, is out of her mind with worry."

"Then you're just going to have to badger her on her phone and via email," Sophie said. "If you do that often enough, she won't forget you."

Pippa stared at her for a long moment. "I like that idea," she said. "I'll send her photos of Amelie every day. She can't ignore me forever."

"Good plan," Sophie said. "And if you want to copy those photos to me, I'd be delighted."

"I shall do that," Pippa said. "Now Bridget has said there's a charity event she's organized with Max. Will you be attending?"

Sophie gave a reluctant nod and took another bite of her dinner. "Of course."

"With whom will you be attending?" Pippa asked with an innocent expression.

"Um, I believe I'll be attending with Max."

Pippa eyes rounded. "Oh, really."

"I think he wants to present solidarity from the company."

"Oh," Pippa said and took another bite of her food. "I suppose that's a good idea."

"I think so," Sophie confirmed. "He wants all of us to help with the project, so other employees will also be attending."

"Good," Pippa said. "With Bridget at the helm, I'm sure it will be a smashing success."

The following Saturday, Sophie helped at the handicapped center, but by afternoon, everyone was released. She took advantage of the extra time to visit a few stores. At one shop, she found a midnight-blue halter dress that was somehow both sensual and understated. Since it was on sale, she bought it right away and decided to ask advice about accessories from Bridget or Pippa or anyone, because accessories were not her forte.

The only thing that was worrying her was the fact that she hadn't started her period, and she was over two weeks late. Sophie was as regular as rain when it came to her menstrual cycle. She and Max had been careful. Most of the time. *Had they missed a few?* she asked herself. *Oh, please no,* she thought. She hoped not.

Sophie lasted through the weekend and the next week, but by next Friday, she was sweating it. *Why was she so late?*

She paced her apartment for a half-hour then went to the pharmacy to pick up a double pregnancy test. She immediately took the test and waited for the results.

Sophie was pregnant.

She kept it to herself for the next week. It was easy because Max was slammed with work. By the time Friday arrived, she collapsed at her apartment and he collapsed at his. On Saturday, she got a mani-pedi and visited a hairstylist. Unfortunately, she hadn't asked for advice on accessories from anyone, so she was on her own.

After her hair appointment, Sophie returned to her apartment and slapped on a little more eye makeup than usual and applied lip gloss. She hoped this would work. Stepping into sandals, she smoothed down her dress and prayed everything would turn out well. Seconds later, her doorbell rang.

Her stomach clenched and she walked to the door and opened it. "Hi," she said, opening the door.

"Wow," Max said, wearing a dark suit, white shirt and red tie. "You look hot."

She couldn't resist a smile. "So do you."

The benefit was a whirlwind. Max laughed and gambled. Sophie did, too, although she wasn't much of a gambler. Waiters kept offering her champagne and booze, but after the pregnancy tests she'd taken, she couldn't imbibe.

She wondered when she would be able to tell Max. She wondered how upset he would be. Not tonight, she told herself. He had too much going on tonight. Perhaps tomorrow? Coming from behind him, she heard him talking to the head of a construction company.

"We're just friends," he said. "I make sure all women know where I stand. I'm committed to being uncommitted when it comes to romantic relationships."

Sophie's heart sank. It didn't take a genius to suspect that Max was speaking about her. He wasn't at all serious about her. She should have known that from the beginning. She *had* known it from the beginning, but she'd ignored it and stuck her head in the ground. How could she possibly tell him that she was carrying his baby?

He would be furious. She wondered if he would even ask her to give up the baby.

The prospect made her so ill she was forced to go to the ladies' room. She barely escaped losing her dinner, took a few breaths and splashed some cool water on her cheeks.

Out of the corner of her eye, she saw Princess Bridget enter the powder room. Sophie gave a quick curtsey. "Your highness."

"A pleasure to see you," Bridget said and winked. "Nice dress, but I still love the red one the best." Bridget studied Sophie and frowned. "Are you okay? You look extremely pale."

Sophie nodded. "I got too warm and it felt too stuffy. I just needed some air and I'm going to get a nice cool glass of water."

"Are you sure you're not ill? I've never seen you this pale, not even in the hospital," Bridget said, worry creasing her brow.

"I'm fine. We've all been working long hours this week. I'll make sure to sleep in tomorrow morning. You're so sweet to ask," Sophie said and was determined to take the attention away from herself. "The casino night is a total success. You're a miracle worker."

Bridget shrugged, but smiled. "Oh, I can't take credit. Several people came through," she said, attempting modesty. "But it is going fabulously, isn't it?"

"Yes, it is," Sophie said. "Now I'm going to let you powder your nose while I get a drink of water. I'll see you later."

"Yes," Bridget said. "Don't overdo. I may have to say something to Maxwell."

"Oh, no. Not necessary," Sophie said, but Bridget had already disappeared into the inner toilet area. Sophie prayed Bridget wouldn't say anything. She didn't want to draw any extra attention to herself. Getting a glass of water from one of the staff, Sophie slinked back against the wall. Even after pulling herself from the crowd, the sights and sounds of the party felt overwhelming.

"Are you all right?" a familiar male voice asked her. "You look pale."

Sophie glanced at David. She hadn't spoken to him

since she'd told him she just wanted to be friends. "I just got a little warm. I'm fine. How are you?"

He gave a charming smile. "Aside from missing your company, I'm well. Are you sure there's nothing I can do for you?"

"Not a thing," she said. "I'm just going to hold up this wall for a few minutes and watch the show."

"As you wish," he said. "Good night, Sophie."

He walked away and she felt a sliver of relief and regret at the same time. It would have been so convenient if she could have fallen for him romantically. He seemed like such a nice man.

Seconds later, she caught sight of Max walking toward her with a tight expression on his face. "I saw Rinaldo talking with you. What did he want?"

"He just said hello then left," she said.

"Are you sure? Was he bothering you?" he asked.

Sophie laughed. "David's too polite to bother me. I told him weeks ago that I wanted to be friends and he has respected that."

Max cleared his throat. "Well, that's good."

Sophie couldn't resist playing back the words Max had said just a few moments earlier. "I'm not sure why you're all that concerned about David. You're committed to being uncommitted and you make sure all women know that. Right?"

"You overheard me talking to Al Janton. I told you I was going to explain our presence together tonight as presenting a united front for the company. Al didn't believe me because he figured out you were the one I took to his hot springs. I had to say something to eliminate his curiosity."

"Hmm," she said, too many emotions churning through her. "But it's really the truth, isn't it? You've always said you believed in no-strings affairs. Is that what we have?"

"Why are you asking me this right now?" he asked, tugging at his shirt collar.

"Just curious," she scoffed, feeling her hands turn clammy with fear. "You don't want any strings between us, do you?"

Max frowned. "Sophie, I know I'd be a rotten husband. I don't want to subject you to that. You deserve better."

"Then why did you get involved with me this way?" she demanded.

"Because I couldn't resist you," he admitted. "I wanted you too much." He gave a sigh of exasperation. "Can we discuss this later? I've got to make a speech and be introduced to the crowd again. It's not my favorite thing to do."

"There's no need to discuss anything later," she said and took a sip of water. "Go ahead. I think the event has gone extremely well."

He nodded. "I was hoping we would make enough to not only complete the renovation, but also take care of the upkeep for several years." He looked at her. "Thanks for being here."

He walked toward the center of the room where Bridget stood, holding court. A microphone was handed to one of the hosts of the event. Someone tapped a glass with a spoon, gathering everyone's attention.

"Ladies and gentlemen," the host said. "It's my honor to announce Her Highness, Princess Bridget."

The crowd erupted in applause and Bridget gave a generous smile. "You're too kind." Well, not too kind, she teased. "I'm so grateful for your participation in this unique project that my brother Maxwell Carter has initiated for our community. A center for handicapped children is a long-needed and welcome addition to Chantaine. We are thrilled that Maxwell has found a way to make it happen for us. And you, you are the most generous people in the world to come out and support this cause. Please give yourselves a hand because you certainly deserve it," Bridget said and led the applause.

"I know you're dying to meet the man behind this project. As most of you know, Maxwell has not only launched the project for the community center, he and his company are primarily responsible for the road improvements on the north end of the island. If you've driven in that area, you know that driving on the roads could be extremely dangerous. My family and I are so grateful to Maxwell for all he has contributed for the good of Chantaine. It is my privilege to present to you, Maxwell Carter."

Another round of applause followed. "Thank you. I'm humbled by your enthusiasm and generosity." Max spoke calmly and steadily. "I'm amazed by how quickly Princess Bridget can pull together an event like this. As

I've said many times, if the party requires more than hamburgers and beer, I'm not the best guy to arrange it."

Laughter rippled through the crowd.

"I appreciate your willingness to make this project happen. I'm beginning to understand why the Devereaux family is so committed to the people of Chantaine. You're a very kind and generous people, and I'm pleased to have this opportunity to make your lives a little better. Thank you again."

More applause followed and tears filled Sophie's eyes. Sophie was caught, as she often was, between her admiration and love for Max, and the fact that he was going to break her heart.

Chapter Eleven

"May I bum a ride home?" Sophie asked Terri as she saw the woman and her husband head toward the exit of the crowded ballroom.

"Of course," Terri said. "But why would you want to leave?"

"Raging headache," Sophie said, which was half-true. Mostly, however, her heart was hurting and she didn't know how to handle the next step she would have to take.

"You look pale," Terri said, eyeing her in concern. "Are you sure nothing else is wrong?"

"Of course not," Sophie lied. "The noise level and crowds just got to me."

"If you say so," Terri said, clearly not convinced. "What about Max?"

"Give me a minute and I'll tell him I'm leaving. I'll meet you out front. Is that okay?"

Terri nodded and Sophie scooted through the crowd. It took a bit of jostling, but she made it to his side and tapped his arm. Although a line of people were waiting to meet him, he turned to her. "What's up?"

"I'm hitching a ride with Terri. Raging headache from the crowd," she said.

"I know what you mean. I can take you home," he said.

She shook her head and smiled. "I don't think that would go over well. Look at all the people who bought a ticket so they could meet you."

He shot her a dry look. "Hate to disappoint. I sure as hell don't have Bridget's charm."

"Do your duty," she said. "Your people await."

"I'll call you tomorrow."

"Sure," she said before she escaped through the crowd. The cool air on her face was a relief as she stepped outside the building. She spotted Terri and her husband's car and ran toward it. Scooting inside the backseat, she sank against the seat and closed her eyes.

Terri's husband, Bob, pulled away from the curb. Sophie opened her eyes to find Terri staring at her from the front seat.

"There's something about this I don't like," Terri said. "I've got this weird feeling in my gut."

"Terri," Bob said. "Sophie may not want to hear about your gut right now."

Terri frowned at her husband. "I'm worried about Sophie. What happened? Did Max step out on you?"

"Oh, no," Sophie said. "It's not that."

"Then what is it?" Terri questioned. "Because I know it's something."

The woman had the instincts of a bloodhound and the intuition of a detective.

"Why are you so pale? Are you sick? Are you—"

"No," Sophie said before Terri could ask any more questions. "You know I've been burning the candle at both ends. I just need a good night's sleep and some quiet."

"Humph," Terri grunted. "I don't know. Something just doesn't feel right."

"Can we talk about this another time?"

Terri sighed. "If you say so," she said, shaking her finger at Sophie. "But you better call me if you're sick or something. You know you can count on me, don't you?" she asked.

Sophie nodded and smiled, biting the inside of her cheek to keep from crying. "I do," she said. "I do."

Blessedly, Terri turned around in her seat and Sophie took some deep breaths. The trip to her apartment only took ten minutes, but it felt like hours to Sophie. As Bob pulled alongside her apartment building, she felt a knot form in her throat. She felt so safe with Terri. She wished she could tell someone that she was pregnant, but she knew she couldn't. Not yet.

Sophie swallowed hard and forced a smile. "You two are the best. Thank you so much for the ride home," she said and reached to give both Terri and her husband a kiss on the cheek.

"Okay, sweet girl," Terri said. "You call me tomorrow. If you don't call me, I'll call you."

"Terri, give the girl a break," Bob chided. "She's already got a headache. Don't make it worse."

"Okay," Terri said then lowered her voice. "But I'll call you tomorrow."

"Good night and thanks again," Sophie said as she climbed out of the car and walked to her building. She waved as she entered the door then climbed the steps to her apartment.

Thank goodness this night was over, she thought as she collapsed on the sofa and kicked off her shoes. She just needed to catch her breath then she would drink some water, wash off her makeup and go to bed.

Her mind whirled and her heart raced with fear. She was going to be just like her mother. She was going to have to raise this child alone and live paycheck to paycheck. Sophie told herself to stop thinking. Tonight wasn't the night for it. She wasn't at all rational. If she were rational, then she would remember she had a very nice chunk of savings and after her experience with her current firm, she could find a job anywhere.

Taking a deep breath, she resolved not to think past the next moment. She was just borrowing trouble and worry, as Terri had often said. There was enough trouble today without getting upset about what might or might not happen tomorrow.

She took another deep breath and felt a fraction of

the panic leave her. She would think about it tomorrow, tomorrow and not until then.

Sophie slept through the night and hoped to awaken very late. Preferably, Monday or Tuesday. Instead, the clock read 8:00 a.m. when she got out of bed. She took a long shower and turned on the television to drown out her thoughts. Although she often talked to her mother via Skype on Sundays, she decided to put it off, fearing her mother would somehow know she was pregnant just by hearing her voice. Which was ridiculous.

She ate a healthy breakfast of yogurt and berries and thought about how she would need to start eating more healthfully. After that, she pretended to do a little house-work: cleaned the bathroom, ran the vacuum, dusted.

Her cell rang as she was dusting. Her heart skipped over itself and she prayed it wasn't Max. Glancing at the caller ID, she saw that it was Pippa. What a gift. "Your highness Pippa," Sophie answered.

"Oh, you must stop with the titles. I'm bored out of my mind and still stuck at the palace. I know you attended a wild party last night, but I thought I would take a chance that you would join me for lunch today," Pippa said. "We can eat outside in the gardens if you like."

"It sounds wonderful. What time?" Sophie asked, thrilled at the chance to escape.

"Will one o'clock work for you?" Pippa asked.

"Perfect. I'll see you then," Sophie said. At that point, she turned off her cell phone and took a walk downtown.

It seemed the appropriate thing to do. She picked up two bunches of flowers, one for her and one for Pippa.

Pippa greeted her with open arms at the palace garden where a small table was set. "Look at you. You brought me flowers, you scoundrel. I just wanted your company," she said and lifted them to her nose to inhale their scent. "Delicious."

"They were so beautiful and you've been so welcoming I couldn't resist," Sophie said.

Pippa shot her a wicked smile. "Nic will be shamed when he returns tomorrow. Maybe he'll slow down his traveling."

"I hope so for both of you." Sophie peeked into the baby carrier to see the infant sleeping peacefully. "She's so sweet."

"She's almost perfect," Pippa whispered. "I don't want to say it too loud because poor Eve and Stefan's baby is still suffering from colic, which means Eve and Stefan are suffering, too." She paused a half beat. "I also don't want to jinx anything."

"You're doing a beautiful job," Sophie said. "I'm so glad she's a good baby."

"Well, I'm not sure I had much say over it. I've decided it's all due to naming her after Amelie. The woman was a saint," Pippa said. "Now sit down for our picnic before Amelie awakens."

Sophie sat at the table and munched on salad, roasted chicken, fruit and a slice of bread. The combination of the meal was perfect. "This is great. I would have been eating a peanut-butter sandwich."

"Trust me, I eat one of those every now and then, too," Pippa said. "Some days are just too busy for anything else. Tell me about the wild party last night."

"Bridget did a fabulous job. I'm certain contributions exceeded all expectations. Big crowd. I think some were also curious to meet Max."

"Well, of course they were," Pippa said. "He's come in like a whirlwind, fixing the roads in the north and now establishing a center for the handicapped. Yet, at the same time, he shies away from the press. Everyone is curious. Who is this masked man?" Pippa joked.

"Good point," Sophie said. "It all turned out beautifully."

"I hear you attended with Max," Pippa slyly added.

Sophie's stomach clenched but she managed a nod. "I told you before. He asked me to attend with him to show a united front from the company. They're breathing down his neck for him to finish the job as soon as possible, but since Chantaine is an island, everything takes—"

"Longer," Pippa finished and frowned. "I hope he's not being unduly pressured. Perhaps we should pressure the government to contribute more funds for—"

"No, no," Sophie said, regret filling her. "Please keep that confidential. I didn't mean to say it. I'm so comfortable with you. It just came out."

Pippa paused. "Of course, I'll keep it confidential. I'm honored that you feel safe with me. I feel the same with you."

Sophie took a deep breath and sighed. "Thank you."

"Dessert is chocolate. Are you game?"

Although her stomach was iffy, Sophie was determined not to show it. "It sounds delicious." A staff member brought the warm chocolate soufflé to the table and Sophie took a bite. "Delicious," she said. "I wish I wasn't so full."

"Surely you can eat a few bites more," Pippa insisted.

"Only a few. Would it be gauche to ask for a take-home bag?" Sophie asked.

Pippa laughed. "Not at all."

A muffled cry sounded from the carrier. Amelie had been quiet until now. "May I hold her?" Sophie asked.

"Of course. How can I refuse when I have warm chocolate soufflé?"

Sophie gingerly picked up the baby and held her close. Amelie made another sound.

"You may have to jiggle her a bit. Or walk," Pippa said, taking another biter of the soufflé. "That's what the nanny and I do."

Sophie jiggled the baby and Amelie seemed to settle down. Sophie couldn't help wondering if she would be a good mother. She wanted to be, but she had no clue how. "How is your husband with her?"

"Pretty good until she's hungry. Then he hands her over to me since I'm nursing. I've promised six months, but that's all. She'll get all the benefits against allergies by then."

Sophie stared down into the child's navy eyes. "She seems very observant."

"When she's awake," Pippa said, "she takes in everything."

"Like her mama and daddy," Sophie said with a smile.

"You're very good with her," Pippa said. "I'm sure you'll be a good mom when it's your time."

Sophie doubted that. "We'll see. Not to pry, but I don't get the impression Amelie was planned. If you don't want to answer that, then don't."

"It's no secret that everything was a horrible mess when I first learned I was pregnant," Pippa said. "Nic's mother had just died. He had to take his father back to the States, then his father nearly killed himself during his grief. Nic was determined not to cause a rift between me and my family. Stefan was ready to kill Nic for getting me pregnant. It was a nightmare."

"How did it all work out?" Sophie asked, searching for some hope of her own.

Pippa smiled. "Nic and I love each other. Nothing was going to change that. I was willing to give up my title for him. He was willing to give me up if that would keep me happy, which, of course, wouldn't have."

"Whew, I had no idea," Sophie said.

"Well, you know what they say. True love can make for a bouncy road." She lifted her hands. "Give me my girl and I'll nurse her. She'll be asleep in less than twenty minutes guaranteed."

Pippa discreetly nursed her baby and talked softly to Sophie. "It's better if you talk and I just nod," Pippa said. "Amelie gets distracted and curious."

Sophie laughed. "Okay, I'll try to come up with something. Bridget is quite the social genius, isn't she?" Sophie said more than asked. "I can't believe she was able to get that many people out on such short notice."

"She's quite amazing," Pippa said in a low voice. The baby lifted her head and Pippa rolled her eyes. "Told you," she mouthed silently.

"I think Max was taken aback by how many people were curious about him."

"He doesn't understand that many people consider him royalty even though he may not," Pippa whispered. The baby didn't lift her head from feeding.

"Interesting," Sophie said. "He has no interest in the public attention."

"Good luck with that," Pippa said quietly. She switched sides for nursing. "It's part of the program."

"Max has never been one to go with the program," Sophie said.

"I sense that. I also sense that about you. The two of you have a lot in common."

Sophie immediately shook her head. "Not really. He's bold and adventurous. I'm just a tagalong."

"You underestimate yourself. The reason I know this is because I finally realized that I also underestimated myself. You are stronger than you realize," she whispered. The baby lifted her head. "Done?" Pippa asked, and lifted Amelie to her shoulder. "Amazing how important a burp is. I remember you showed Eve that."

"I learned that when I was a babysitter," Sophie said, still reeling from what Pippa had said. How could the princess possibly know her well enough to say those things?

Just a little while later, Sophie gave Pippa a hug and Amelie a kiss then returned to her apartment. She was glad she'd gotten two bunches of flowers. Her bouquet greeted her with a cheerful appearance and the scent of the carnations wafted throughout the room. She touched them and moved to the kitchen to pour herself a glass of water.

Although she didn't want to do it, she turned on her cell phone. It vibrated with messages. Max. Terri. Max. Max. Sophie sighed. She supposed she would have to call him. Reluctantly pushing his speed-dial button, she waited at the same time she heard a knock at her door.

Her phone against her ear, she went to the door and looked through the peephole. *Max*. She turned off her phone and opened the door.

His expression was dark and cloudy. "Where the hell have you been?"

"Eating lunch with your sister and niece," Sophie said. "Would you like to come in?"

"Eve or Pippa?" he asked.

"Eve had a son and is your sister-in-law," she said. "Pippa is your sister and she had a daughter."

"Okay," he said as he entered the room. "Who gave you the flowers?"

"*Me*. I liked them."

His expression turned mildly sheepish. "Okay. Sorry. I thought something might be wrong after what you said last night. Then you left with Terri and her husband."

Sophie took a deep breath and decided *no time like the present*. "You might want to sit down," she said.

"Why?" he asked a bit rebelliously.

She lowered her voice. "You might want to sit down," she repeated.

Lifting his eyebrows, he sank onto the couch. "What's up?"

"Well," she said as she paced the carpet in front of the couch. "I don't exactly know how to tell you this. I don't want to hear anything negative, but I don't expect anything positive from you."

Max frowned. "What in hell are you talking about?"

His tone irritated her. "You're not the most patient person in the world, are you?"

"As if that's a surprise to you, after the years you've known me," he said.

She grimaced at him. "Again, I don't exactly know..." She took a breath and went to the bathroom, pulled out the last tube of pregnancy results. She brought it back to him. "Two pink lines mean a positive. You're gonna be a daddy."

He stared at her in disbelief. "This can't be possible."

"It is. I took two tests," she said.

"Is there any chance I'm not the father?" he asked.

Rage exploded from insider her. "Get out," she said breathlessly.

"Wait," he said, standing. "It's a legitimate question. You were dating David Rinaldo right before we got—"

"Get out," she screamed.

* * *

Max stumbled out of Sophie's apartment. She'd looked so infuriated he'd thought his life might be in danger. His question about David Rinaldo had been perfectly legitimate. The bastard had been romancing her before he and Sophie had gotten involved. Not only that, Rinaldo had tried to get close to Sophie last night. The sight of the two of them together had made him nuts.

Then the memory made him feel like an idiot. She'd told him she only wanted to be friends with him. He took a deep breath and decided both of them needed some time apart. He couldn't believe the news, he thought as he made his way to his car. She was pregnant.

He was the father.

Every breath he took shook him. *He* was going to be a father. How could that be? He'd always been so careful. Even with Sophie. But maybe not as careful as he'd been with other women. He trusted her. She had always had his back. But is this something that you even leave up to trust? Now, he didn't know what to think.

Max drove to his apartment in a daze. Every time he thought about the fact that Sophie was going to have his baby, he nearly had a heart attack. He had to figure out the best thing to do. He couldn't wing this. It was too important.

Grabbing a beer from his refrigerator, he sat down in a chair and turned on his television. It didn't take much thinking for him to come to a conclusion. He wanted his child to have the best life possible. That meant he and Sophie would have to get married as soon as possible.

He was tempted to return to her apartment right away, but he figured she needed to calm down, too.

Max winced, realizing he hadn't been the most supportive father-to-be. He was going to have to work on her to agree with his plan, but he was determined. He would make it happen.

The next morning, Max waited for Sophie to come into work. But soon enough, he had to solve more than one problem or catastrophe. Midmorning, he walked into the work trailer and she still wasn't there. He turned to Terri. "Where's Sophie?" he asked.

"She called in sick."

Well, hell. "Can't remember the last time she did that," he muttered.

"Me either," Terri said. "She had a super bad headache after the party."

"Yeah," he said.

"I wonder if I should go check on her," she said.

"No. I'll do that after work." And he suspected there would be hell to pay.

Max left work early, went to his place to take a shower then drove to Sophie's apartment. He hoped like hell she was there. He knocked on the door and waited, then knocked again.

Finally the door opened. Sophie wore a pair of black stretch pants and a black top. The dark color only served to emphasize the hollows beneath her eyes. "Hi," he said.

"Hi," she simply replied, her gaze full of reluctance and distrust.

Max hated that, but walked inside her apartment anyway. "I realize I didn't respond well the other night," he admitted.

"You think?" Sophie asked, her arms firmly over her chest.

"Hey, at least you had a chance to work through it before you told me. I had nothing," he said. "Zero seconds."

"Your response was still horrible."

"I agree."

She took a deep breath, but her arms were still closed over her chest.

Max could tell she wasn't going to help him one iota. He supposed he deserved it. "I apologize," he said.

"For what?" she asked.

"For everything. Especially for the way I responded."

She still regarded him skeptically.

"I never thought I would be a father," he said.

"I didn't think I would be a mother at this point either."

He nodded.

"You apparently have super sperm. That's not a compliment," she said.

He nodded again. "Well, we have to deal with the so-called new reality. We're having a baby."

She took a deep breath. "Yes."

"So the only choice is that we should get married."

Sophie blinked, but said nothing.

"Did you hear what I said?" he asked.

She nodded slowly.

"We need to get married. I want my child to have the

best future possible. The only way to accomplish that is for you and I to get married."

Sophie nodded again, but the expression in her eyes and her silent replies bothered him.

"So you agree? We'll make it happen as soon as possible," he said.

"Not so fast," Sophie said, catching him by surprise. "I'm going to have to think about this."

Max frowned. "What do you mean you have to think about it?"

"I mean, I'm not sure marriage is the best choice in this case," she said.

"Why in hell would you say that?" he demanded.

"Because you don't want to be married to me or anyone else," she said. "That's why."

And Max couldn't deny it. He was certain he would be the worst husband ever.

Chapter Twelve

Sophie went to work the next day. Terri grilled her like she was a hamburger at a barbecue.

"I don't want to talk about it," she said to Terri.

"What did Max do? I'll give him a good tongue-lashing. I'm betting he needs it," she said.

Sophie laughed. "I love you for your vivacity," she said, putting her hand on Terri's arm. "But let me deal with this."

Terri frowned. "I don't like this."

"You always said I was stronger than I thought I was," Sophie told Terri.

Terri paused for a long moment. "I did, but I never wanted you to have to be so strong."

"I'm okay," Sophie said. That was a lie, but she was getting there. She would get there. She was sure of it.

A half moment later, Max strode into the trailer. He looked up and stared at her, stunned. "What are you doing here?" he said more than asked.

"I work here."

He opened his mouth to say something then wisely chose to close it.

"How's it going?" Sophie asked.

"Fine," he replied shortly.

"Terrible," Terri said. "Supplies are late."

"That sucks," Sophie said. "I'll get on the phone."

"You don't have to do that," Max said.

"Yes, I do. I work here."

Sophie got on the line and chewed out their supplier. Good news, they arrive this afternoon. She was gratified by Max's surprised reaction.

"How'd you do that?" he asked.

"I was very firm," she said.

"I was firm," he said.

"I was firm to the right person. Plus I promised I would send her Fat Witch Brownies."

He frowned in confusion. "Who is this person?"

Sophie shrugged. "I'm sorry. I can't reveal my sources at this time."

He scowled at her. "What?"

"Later," she said. "I can tell you more later. Just be glad you've gotten supplies."

"What are Fat Witch Brownies?" he asked. "They sound horrible."

"They're delicious and wonderful. You have to find

the sweet spot of the person who can help you. Brownies work for this particular person."

"You're sneakier than I thought you were," he said.

"I'm not sneaky. I just try to meet needs, negotiate terms and make things happen."

He met her gaze. "I always knew you were smart."

"So did I," she said. "I just want to be smarter and stronger than I've ever been. I have to be," she said.

Sophie could see that Max hadn't truly realized all she'd done to help facilitate his projects until this moment. That was okay. She knew he was the visionary and she found ways to make things happen.

"We all have our strengths," she said. "You've always said that."

"Yeah. I just never realized the extent of yours," he said.

"That's okay," she said and smiled. "A lot of people have underestimated me."

He opened his mouth to protest then slowly closed it. A confession that he, too, had underestimated her. *But maybe not by very much,* she thought.

Sophie worked past quitting time then drove back to her apartment. She was going to have to figure out a new work/life balance. After eating a healthy meal, she put on comfy clothes, sank into her sofa and turned on her TV. She didn't much care what she watched. She just wanted to escape.

Gradually sinking against her pillow, she heard a knock at her door nearly an hour later. Sophie reluctantly rose from the sofa and went to the door. She looked out the peephole. Max with a bouquet of flowers.

Reluctantly, she opened the door. "I was asleep."

"Sorry. Here," he said, pushing the flowers into her hand while striding inside.

Sophie sighed and took the flowers to the kitchen to put them in a pitcher. Afterward, she returned to the den. "Thank you, but I'm going to bed soon. What did you want?" she asked.

"I want you to marry me," he said firmly. "It's the best thing for our child. I want to do the best thing for our baby."

She bit her lip. "A marriage isn't just about the baby," she said. "It's about the man and woman, too."

"What's most important?" Max asked. "The baby or the adults?"

"They're all important. No one should feel trapped. No one should feel as if they're making a big sacrifice. That wouldn't be good for the baby or the adults," she said.

He frowned. "Sophie, I'm not joking. This is important."

"I agree," she said dryly. "It's important for at least three people."

"How can I convince you that you and I getting married is the right thing to do?"

Sophie's stomach clenched. She moved toward him. "I need more than an obligatory baby daddy."

"Obligatory?" he echoed.

"Yes," Sophie said. "Can you honestly say that you

would have asked me to marry you if I weren't pregnant?"

She met his gaze for a long moment and saw the truth written across his face. It broke her heart. Not for the first time.

"A child changes things," he said. "A child changes the way you look at life."

"I agree," she said. "Before now, I would have been thrilled for you to propose marriage to me. I would have given everything for that to happen. But now, I know I want more. I want a man who wants me. Not just our baby."

"You know I want you," he said.

She shrugged. "What you wanted more than anything was a *no-strings* relationship with me. I know that about you. If you told me once, you told me a hundred times. You don't want to be a family man, and I don't want to be the person to try and make you be a family man."

He raked his hand through his hair. "I don't know what to say."

She shook her head. "There's nothing to say. I will handle this. It's what women do."

"You don't have to do it alone," he said, his body emanating conviction. "I'll be there for you."

She lifted her shoulders. "Okay," she said, but she knew she didn't sound very convincing. She didn't believe that Max truly wanted to be there for her.

Max was summoned to the palace to have a drink with Stefan. The purpose for the meeting was the same:

a status update on road construction. In Max's timetable, he'd hoped to be finished by now.

Max was led to Stefan's office where the prince was seated at his desk, wearing casual clothes. Max couldn't recall a time he'd seen Stefan, always Mr. Business, wearing anything but a suit. "Please, come in," he said to Max, waving him toward the desk. "This was supposed to be a day off, but you know what happens to those when your office is so close. Whiskey?"

"I'll just take water tonight," Max said.

"Okay," Stefan said and nodded toward his assistant. "Please bring our guest some water. I'll have the same." He turned back to Max. "I hear from Bridget that the charity event was quite successful."

"It was," Max said. "Your sister knows how to throw a party and get people to open their wallets."

"Yes, it's a special, but sometimes undervalued, skill. My wife tells me I should praise Bridget more often," Stefan said. The assistant served the water. "Thank you."

"How are your wife and new son?" Max asked.

"Kind of you to ask," Stefan said. "My wife is a bit tired from dealing with our son. He still has colic. Eve says he has an arsenic hour or two every day. The doctor says it will pass. If it doesn't kill us first," Stefan muttered.

"I'm sorry the baby's giving you a rough time," Max said, thinking about how he would react to his own crying baby when the time came. The thought unsettled him.

"Thank you. We'll manage. I'm glad Eve will allow

the nannies to occasionally help. In the beginning, she insisted that she had to do everything for him. It left her exhausted. I had to insist that she take a break. She was very unhappy with me. She thought I didn't believe she could be a good enough mother. It's a tricky line to walk with new mothers. But I'm sure I've told you more than you wanted to know," Stefan drifted off.

"I wouldn't have asked if I weren't interested," Max said.

Stefan nodded. "Thank you, then. The reason I invited you was to ask about the progress on the road construction."

"Slower than I had hoped or planned. I've made a revised schedule that should add another four weeks to the original finish date," Max said, tamping down his frustration.

"That's still quite impressive," Stefan said. "Our last road construction project took over a year."

"That standard won't work for me or my company," Max said and took a drink of water.

"I understand about having high standards. Eve is constantly reminding me that even Superman takes a break every now and then," Stefan said.

"It's true, but you're not just fighting your everyday battles," Max said. "You're fighting an image battle, too."

"Yes, it's important that people know we're not a bunch of royals living off the people and doing nothing," he said.

"The opposite of how Prince Edward presented himself," Max mused. Even though Max didn't think of Prince Edward as his father, he could imagine what a looming figure the man could have been to Stefan. "When did you decide to be different?"

"Truth?" Stefan asked. "I think I was born different. My father didn't like to study. I enjoyed learning, and having a feeling of accomplishment. There was a period of time when I resented my father for his lifestyle, but as I've matured, I can't deny that he did some good things. One of which was to help produce my sisters and brother, who have all turned out very well. Look at you and Coco. Even his infidelities produced good people."

"That's forward thinking of you," Max said with a half grin.

"Better than backward," Stefan said. "At several points in my life, I came to the conclusion that I didn't want to be defined by my father's actions. I wanted to be defined by my own actions. It was—" He paused then nodded. "Liberating."

"Sounds like it," Max said. Stefan had given him a lot of food for thought.

"Yes. I've gone philosophical on you," Stefan said and chuckled. "Enough of that. What I wanted to tell you is that I realize that the cost of the road construction has increased. Your company has been quite generous, but perhaps a word with one of our government officials would be in order. Chantaine should be able to contribute more to the cause if necessary."

"It's not necessary," Max said. "I made a promise and I'll make it happen."

Stefan gave a slow nod. "If you should change your mind—"

"Would you?" Max asked.

Stefan met his gaze and Max saw a glint of respect mingling with humor. "When you put it like that." Stefan rose and extended his hand. "Try not to kill yourself, Max."

"No chance. I like a challenge," he said and shook Stefan's hand.

"We'd like you to join us for dinner sometime soon," Stefan said. "My assistant will call to set up a time."

The invitation took him off guard. "Okay," he said. "I work late most evenings, though."

"As Eve would say, you have to eat sometime. We'll work something out," Stefan said.

Max left the palace and returned to his apartment, his mind full of what Stefan had said about his father. Stefan had clearly made a deliberate choice to be different. He wanted to be a better leader for the people of Chantaine, so he did it. He wanted to be a better husband, a better brother, a better father.

Max's respect for Stefan grew as he thought about how much he had overcome. If Stefan had decided he could be different from the example his father had given him, then maybe Max could be different, too. After all, he wasn't a complete dunce. He could learn. He thought about Sophie and knew he had an uphill climb trying to persuade her that he even *wanted* to be the dependable man she wanted and the good father their baby needed, let alone be that person.

Sighing, he raked his hand through his hair. This wasn't the first time he'd faced a challenge. He would prove to her that he was the right man to be her husband and the father of their child. He was determined.

Max quickly learned that he might be determined, but Sophie was no pushover in this area. It was as if the knowledge of her pregnancy had turned her spine to steel and while she was polite to him, she'd put up a wall between them. The tables had turned. In the past, he'd compartmentalized, insisting that he keep their relationship friendly but all business. Now she was treating him the same way.

She performed her work duties better than ever, but once she left that work trailer, she tolerated his presence, but not much more. He brought her flowers and meals. She said thank you, chatted with him for a bit then showed him the door.

One night, his frustration got the best of him. "What is it going to take for you to let me back into your life?" he asked as he sat across from her in her den.

She blinked. "You're in my life," she said. "You're just not in my bed. I don't think it's a good idea for an expecting mother to be having a no-strings affair with a man, even if that man is her baby's father."

"But I've told you I don't want a no-strings affair. I want to marry you," he said, grinding his teeth.

"And the prospect makes you so happy you can hardly stand it." She rolled her eyes sarcastically.

Offended by her lighthearted response when he was

dead serious about the issue, he frowned. "I'm unhappy because you won't take my proposal seriously."

"Do we have to talk about this again?" Sophie asked. "I know where you stand. You know where I stand. Every time you bring it up, it makes us both miserable."

"So you just want us to continually dance around the subject? You know that's not my way."

"Yes, but I'm not going to change my mind just because that's what you want," she said.

Impatience chapped at him. "I just want to take care of you and our child. Is that so horrible?"

Her face softened. "Not at all. I'm just afraid that at some point, you'll come to your senses and resent me or the baby. I couldn't bear it if that happened."

"It won't happen," he said, but he could see by her expression that he had much more work to do.

Sophie started taking a yoga class to offset her anxiety. Terri was still hounding her at work and Max was hounding her in the evenings. She hadn't told anyone except Max about the pregnancy, but she knew she couldn't hide it forever. At some point, she would need to make plans. It was odd to consider the reality of not working with Max, of choosing a place to live and making a home for her and her child.

Bridget called her after one of her yoga classes. "We're having another picnic at the palace. Eve, Pippa and I would love for you to join us. I must warn you that all the hooligans will be there. My boys, Stephenia and the babies. No men except for my little ones. Will you come?"

Sophie enjoyed the craziness of the royal sisters and was still surprised by how much they'd included her. If and when she left Chantaine, she would miss them terribly. "I'd love to. It sounds like fun." A nice escape from her own worries.

Arriving at the palace, she parked her car and walked toward the play area where she'd been told to meet everyone. The twins and Stephenia were already climbing and running. Bridget stood guard, wearing slacks and her ever present heels. Eve had her baby strapped to the front of her and Pippa's little sweetheart was propped in her carrier.

Eve caught sight of her first. "There you are, you brave soul," she said with a smile.

Pippa turned and waved. "Come watch the action."

Bridget shot Sophie a sly glance. "Best form of birth control ever," she joked.

The comment gave her a jolt and she automatically covered her abdomen with her hand. Did Bridget know? Of course she didn't, she told herself. She was just being paranoid.

Eve gave a loud sound of disapproval. "You're going to have a baby someday and you'll be eating your words."

"I was just kidding," Bridget said. "You know I love my hooligans. Travis, stop pulling on Stephenia's dress," she called.

"You're such a natural, Bridget," Pippa said. "You should have at least a dozen."

Bridget stared her sister in horror. "Now who's joking?"

"You two need to stop. We're frightening Sophie," Eve said.

"Not at all," Sophie said. "This is the best entertainment I've had all week." She glanced at Eve. "You're looking good. If I didn't know you'd had a baby several weeks ago, I wouldn't guess it now."

"I haven't lost all the pregnancy weight, but I'm getting more sleep. Plus, we've used your massage technique on June Bug and also figured out that putting the baby in this little pouch keeps him from getting so cranky. I swear it's magic. Stefan wants to give the inventor a special royal commendation."

"Good for you," Sophie said, mentally taking notes. "He has really grown," she said and glanced at Pippa who was gently rocking the baby carrier. "I see Amelie is her regular sweet self."

Pippa nodded. "As good as gold. I have a feeling things may change once she starts moving around, so I'm going to enjoy this easy stage."

"Everyone ready to eat?" Bridget asked both the children and the adults.

"Yes," the little ones chorused.

"Let's wash hands first," Eve said.

The children ran toward the small building next to the playground that housed a kitchen and restroom. A nanny stood at the door waiting to help them. Soon after, a staff member brought the food to the table. Chicken drumsticks for the children and roasted chicken breast and salad for the adults.

"I understand you and Max have been working very hard on the road project," Eve said.

"Everyone is," Sophie said. "It's taking a little longer than planned and Max isn't used to that. He takes pride in beating deadlines."

"It's a different animal when you're dealing with an island. I'm sure it's frustrating."

"It is, but we'll work through it and the road will be built. There are usually bumps, just not this many."

"I don't like to think about you leaving," Pippa said. "Do you have any idea where you'll be assigned once this contract is complete? I wonder if we could find a job for you here in Chantaine."

"Thank you. I've enjoyed my time here, too," she said and felt the sudden sting of sadness. "I'll miss all of you terribly," she said, surprised when her voice broke. "I'm sorry," she said. "That came out of nowhere, didn't it?"

Pippa patted her hand. "We feel the same way," she said. "You've become such a good friend to us."

Eve and Bridget murmured their agreement.

"Well, I say we don't have to think about this now," Bridget said. "Not when the staff is bringing chocolate cake for everyone."

"Can't argue with that," Eve said.

The chocolate cake was served and Sophie was pretty sure the children got more of it on them than in them, but perhaps that was part of the plan. More wash-ups commenced and after the nannies took the children up to the nurseries, Sophie took her turn in the restroom.

She saw spots of blood on her panties and fear rushed through her. She stepped out of the restroom and immediately grabbed her cell phone. Her hands shaking, she punched in her speed dial for Max.

"Sophie, what's wrong? You look live you've seen a ghost," Bridget said.

Max's number went straight to voice mail and Sophie's sense of panic nearly went out of control. "I need to talk to Max. There's blood. The baby."

Pippa's eyes rounded. "Baby!" She rose from the table. "Quick, we need to get her in the palace. She needs to lie down."

"And we need to get to Max. Where is he?" Bridget asked.

"Probably working at the center for handicapped children if he's not at the office trailer," Sophie said, so scared. What if she was losing the baby?

Max continued to saw the wood into the correct dimensions to widen the door frame leading into the center for handicapped children. A tap on his shoulder got his attention and he stopped working. Turning around, he recognized the man as a palace aide. "Gerard," he said, remembering the man's name. "Can I help you with something?"

"I'm afraid there may be a problem, Mr. Carter," Gerard said. "Miss Taylor is asking for you. She's at the palace."

His heart fell to his feet. "Sophie. Is she okay? Is everything okay?"

"We're not sure, sir. That's why you need to come right away."

Max immediately left with the aide. His mind was running a mile a minute. "Does she need medical attention?" he hastily asked Gerard.

"The palace physician is on his way," Gerard said.

"Won't she need a full-staffed hospital?" Max said. "Do you know what happened?"

"Princess Bridget mentioned something about a baby and spotting. I'm sorry I can't tell you more. I was asked to bring you back to the palace as soon as possible."

The drive felt as if it were taking forever. All the while, Max wondered how Sophie was. He didn't know much about pregnancy, but he didn't want her life in danger. He wanted her safe and the baby safe.

The terrible thought of losing her stabbed at him. Her accident with the scooter had shaken him up badly, but this, this was different. The prospect of not having her in his life made him crazy.

"Can you go any faster?" he asked the driver.

"I'm over the limit, sir. I'll get you there as soon as I possibly can."

The car finally arrived at the palace and Max stepped out before it came to a complete stop. "Where is she?" he asked Gerard.

"I'll take you," he said, moving quickly to a side entrance. Max followed the man up a flight of stairs and down a hallway to a room where several people stood outside.

"Please step aside," Gerard said to the staff members and knocked on the door then opened it. "Mr. Carter."

Max rushed into the room to find Sophie lying on the bed. The look of fear on her face tore at him. "Sophie," he said, moving to her side.

"Oh, Max, thank God you're here," she said, her voice coming out in a sob.

He pulled her against him. "What happened? Are you okay?"

"I had some spotting and I didn't know what it meant. I'm afraid I'm losing the baby," she said as her eyes welled up with tears.

Max felt so helpless he couldn't stand it. "Where's the doctor?" he asked, looking around, suddenly noticing that Pippa and Bridget were also in the room.

"She's already been examined," Bridget said. "The doctor is bringing in an ultrasound machine on loan. It should be here any moment."

"I don't want to lose your baby," Sophie said. "I don't—" She buried her head in his shoulder and more than anything Max wanted to hold her and protect her. And love her forever.

"I love you," he said. "I don't want to lose you."

She lifted her head, her beautiful brown eyes filled with tears and surprise. "What?" she whispered.

"I love you. I want this baby, too," he said, feeling as if a vise had tightened around his heart and throat. "But whatever happens about the baby, I love you, Sophie. I need you in my life. I don't want to spend one day of my life without you in it."

"Oh, Max." She closed her eyes and tears spilled down her cheeks. "I was afraid to even dream you would ever say those words to me. I didn't think it was possible."

"I've been fighting it a long time," he said. "I can't fight it anymore. Please marry me."

She stared at him in wonder and drew a shaky breath. "I believe you," she said. "I can't say no. Not anymore. Yes, I'll marry you."

Max felt relief shoot through him, warming and softening his heart.

There was a knock on the door and Max glanced over his shoulder.

"The doctor's here with the ultrasound machine," Bridget said, pushing aside a few tears of her own. "Are you ready?"

Max looked at Sophie. "Ready?" he asked.

"I'm scared," she said, reaching for his hand.

"We can handle anything if we're together," he assured her.

She took a deep breath and nodded. The doctor came inside the room and Bridget introduced him to Max while he set up the machine.

"I'll put gel on your abdomen and try to get a good picture of what's going on. Remember, I told you that many women spot and still go on to deliver healthy babies. It's still worth checking, though."

The doctor proceeded with the exam, moving the

probe over Sophie's abdomen. "Hmm, hmm," he said then smiled. "Would you like to see your baby's heartbeat? Very strong," he said, swiveling the monitor so that both Max and Sophie could see it.

"Your baby is quite tiny at this stage, but the heartbeat is very healthy. Everything looks good."

"Oh, thank goodness," Sophie said, her voice full of relief. She met Max's gaze. "I love you," she said. "And I'm so happy that I'm going to have your baby."

Epilogue

*Two months later... *

Max stood on a private beach in Chantaine with a minister beside him. Max was waiting for Sophie. He realized he'd been waiting for Sophie since he was born. Now, he was waiting to bind himself to her forever.

He'd spent a lifetime keeping people at arm's length, but Sophie had burrowed her way into his heart, thank goodness. He couldn't remember a time when he'd felt more at peace, more excited about his personal future. He had even allowed himself to get a little closer to the Devereauxes. He didn't exactly know how to be a brother, but he could learn. Sophie was helping him learn a lot of things about himself.

She finally appeared over the crest of the hill. His

heart caught at the sight of her. Her unruly hair was pulled partly back, but the rest of her curls tumbled over her shoulders. The slight breeze blew at the hem of her ivory dress that showed just a hint of her baby bump.

Every cell in his body knew her as his mate. There was no denying that fact. As she walked toward him, her lips lifted in a big smile that turned him upside down.

She crossed the sand to stand in front of him, clutching her bouquet of flowers in her hands. He hoped she wasn't nervous. He hoped she knew how important she was to him.

He reached out to take her hand. The move was unscripted, but he wanted her to feel his reassurance. She wasn't in this alone. He was in it all the way with her.

"Dearly beloved," the minister began, following with Max's vows. Then Sophie made hers.

What had been true for years finally became official.

"You may kiss your bride," he said and Max pulled Sophie into his arms and kissed her long and hard.

The guests applauded, but he could barely hear them over the joy in his heart.

Sophie was flying high by the time she and Max made a quick stop at their new cottage in between the wedding and reception. She couldn't stop laughing.

"We did it," she said to him as they walked to the front porch. "We did it."

"We did," he said. "And it's only going to get better."

"I'm so glad we were married on the beach. It was perfect," she said. "Especially since we're planning to stay in Chantaine for a while."

"My *sisters,*" he said, the word still feeling strange on his tongue, "did a great job helping you plan. Bet you had to rein in Bridget."

"Of course we did. I'm just so pleased Coco and her family were able to come. I finally got to meet her before the ceremony. Now I understand why everyone says she's such a sweetheart."

"Good people, all of them," Max said. "That's something Stefan said awhile back to me about all of us. He's right."

"They've been so welcoming to me. I really do feel like part of the family," she said. "And have you noticed that your mother and mine are getting along like two peas in a pod? I overheard both of them talking about moving to a retirement community in Florida. Wouldn't that be amazing?"

"We'll see," he said and swung her into his arms as he stepped into the cottage. "The only thing I'm hearing from my mother is that she is coming back to Chantaine once you have the baby." That second a dog bounded toward them and wagged its tail. Max gently set Sophie down.

She bent to pet the dog. "I can't believe how wonderfully it's all turned out. You, me, our baby on the way and my very own King Charles spaniel puppy. That was the best wedding gift you could give me. I feel like the luckiest woman in the world."

Max pulled her into his arms. "And I plan to keep you feeling that way. Forever," he promised.

* * * * *

#2251 HER HIGHNESS AND THE BODYGUARD
The Bravo Royales
Christine Rimmer
Princess Rhiannon Bravo-Calabretti has loved only one man in her life—orphan turned soldier Captain Marcus Desmarais—but he walked away knowing that she deserved more than a commoner. Years later, fate stranded them together overnight in a freak spring blizzard...and gave them an unexpected gift!

#2252 TEN YEARS LATER...
Matchmaking Mamas
Marie Ferrarella
Living in Tokyo, teaching English, Sebastian Hunter flees home to his suddenly sick mother's side just in time to attend his high school reunion. Brianna MacKenzie, his first love, looks even better than she had a decade ago...but can he win her over for the second and final time?

#2253 MARRY ME, MENDOZA
The Fortunes of Texas: Southern Invasion
Judy Duarte
Because of a stipulation in her employment contract, Nicole Castleton needs to marry before she can become the CEO of Castleton Boots. Her plan to reunite with ex–high school sweetheart Miguel Mendoza was strictly business—until their hearts got in the way!

#2254 A BABY IN THE BARGAIN
The Camdens of Colorado
Victoria Pade
After what her great-grandfather did to his family, bitter Gideon Thatcher refuses to hear a word of January Camden's apology...or get close to the beautiful brunette. Plus, she's desperate to have a baby, and Gideon does *not* see children in his future. But after spending time together, they may find they share more than just common ground....

#2255 THE DOCTOR AND MR. RIGHT
Rx for Love
Cindy Kirk
Dr. Michelle Kerns has a "no kids" rule when it comes to dating men...until she meets her hunky neighbor who has a child—a thirteen-year-old girl to be exact! Her mind says no, but maybe this one rule *is* meant to be broken!

#2256 THE TEXAN'S FUTURE BRIDE
Byrds of a Feather
Sheri WhiteFeather
Suffering from amnesia, J.D. wandered aimlessly through Buckshot Hills until Jenna Byrd offered the injured cowboy a place to stay. Slowly memories flood back to him, but what he remembers makes him want to run away from love—*fast*. Yet why can't he keep himself out of beautiful Jenna's embrace?

*She thought she was free of Marcus forever—until
he turned up as her unexpected bodyguard at
her sister's wedding!*

*Read on for a sneak peek at the next installment
of Christine Rimmer's bestselling miniseries*
THE BRAVO ROYALES....

***

How could this have happened?

Rhiannon Bravo-Calabretti, Princess of Montedoro, could
not believe it. Honestly. What were the odds?

One in ten, maybe? One in twenty? She supposed that
it could have been just the luck of the draw. After all, her
country was a small one and there were only so many rigor-
ously trained bodyguards to be assigned to the members of
the princely family.

However, when you added in the fact that Marcus Desmarais wanted nothing to do with her ever again, reason-
able odds became pretty much no-way-no-how. Because he
would have said no.

So why hadn't he?

A moment later she realized she knew why: because if he
refused the assignment, his superiors might ask questions.
Suspicion and curiosity could be roused, and he wouldn't
have wanted that.

Stop.

Enough. Done. She was simply not going to think about
it—about *him*—anymore.

She needed to focus on the spare beauty of this beautiful wedding in the small town of Elk Creek, Montana. Her sister was getting married. Everyone was seated in the little church.

Still, *he* would be standing. In back somewhere by the doors, silent and unobtrusive. Just like the other security people. Her shoulders ached from the tension, from the certainty he was watching her, those eerily level, oh-so-serious, almost-green eyes staring twin holes in the back of her head.

It doesn't matter. Forget about it, about him.

It didn't matter why he'd been assigned to her. He was there to protect her, period. And it was for only this one day and the evening. Tomorrow she would fly home again. And be free of him. Forever.

She could bear anything for a single day. It had been a shock, that was all. And now she was past it.

She would simply ignore him. How hard could that be?

***

Don't miss HER HIGHNESS AND THE BODYGUARD, coming in April 2013 in Harlequin® Special Edition®.

*And look for Alice's story,
HOW TO MARRY A PRINCESS, only from
Harlequin® Special Edition®, in November 2013.*

HSEEXP0313

SPECIAL EDITION

Life, Love and Family

There's magic—and love—in those Texas hills!

THE TEXAN'S FUTURE BRIDE
by Sheri WhiteFeather

Suffering from amnesia, J.D. wandered aimlessly through Buckshot Hills until Jenna Byrd offered the injured cowboy a place to stay. Slowly memories seep back to him, but what he remembers makes him want to run away from love—*fast*. Yet why can't he keep himself out of beautiful Jenna's embrace?

Look for the second title in the *Byrds of a Feather* miniseries next month!

Available in April 2013 from Harlequin Special Edition wherever books are sold.

www.Harlequin.com

HSE65738

SPECIAL EDITION

Life, Love and Family

Looking for your next
Fortunes of Texas: Southern Invasion fix?

Coming next month
MARRY ME, MENDOZA
by Judy Duarte

Because of a stipulation in her employment
contract, Nicole Castleton needs to marry before
she can become the CEO of Castleton Boots.
Her plan to reunite with former high school
sweetheart Miguel Mendoza was strictly
business—until their hearts got in the way!

*Available in April 2013 from Harlequin Special Edition
wherever books are sold.*

It all starts with a kiss

Check out the brand-new series

HARLEQUIN® KISS™

Fun, flirty and sensual romances.
ON SALE JANUARY 22!

HARLEQUIN®

A *Romance* FOR EVERY MOOD™

Stay up-to-date on all your
romance-reading news with the
Harlequin Shopping Guide,
featuring bestselling authors, exciting new
miniseries, books to watch and more!

The newest issue will be delivered right to you
with our compliments! There are 4 each year.

Signing up is easy.

EMAIL

ShoppingGuide@Harlequin.ca

WRITE TO US

HARLEQUIN BOOKS
Attention: Customer Service Department
P.O. Box 9057, Buffalo, NY 14269-9057

OR PHONE

1-800-873-8635 in the United States
1-888-343-9777 in Canada

Please allow 4-6 weeks for delivery of the first issue by mail.